Praise for

Belle Prater's Boy

A Newbery Honor Book
An ALA Best Book for Young Adults
An ALA Notable Book
A *Boston Globe–Horn Book* Honor Book
A *School Library Journal* Best Book of the Year
A *Publishers Weekly* Best Book of the Year
An IRA Teachers' Choice
An NCSS/CBC Notable Children's Trade Book in the Field of Social Studies
Recipient of a *Parenting* Magazine Reading Magic Award

★"White paints a vivid picture of small-town Appalachia in the 1950s. . . . Characterization is superb. . . . White's message—that there is no protection for any of us from pain, only a variety of ways to handle it—is delivered with just right dollops of humor and love. . . . A delightful read by a real truth teller."
—*School Library Journal*, Starred

★"Pitching her narrative in a genial, mountain-folks twang, White creates vivacious, memorable characters whose openheartedness should not be mistaken for näiveté. She gives her protagonists the courage to face tragedy and transcend it—and the ability to pass along that gift to the reader." —*Publishers Weekly*, Starred

"Ruth White creates a satisfying feeling of community. . . . An admirable, stirring book." —*The New York Times Book Review*

"White's characters are strong—and her storytelling is rich in detail and emotion."
—*The Horn Book Magazine*

"Both central and secondary characters are vividly realized in a plot that draws on family dynamics for its tension and energy. . . . White knows her setting well enough to poke fun without sacrificing her affection for the small-town atmosphere."
—*The Bulletin*, Recommended

Ruth White is the author of *Sweet Creek Holler*, an ALA Notable Book, and *Weeping Willow*, an ALA Best Book for Young Adults. She lives in Virginia Beach, Virginia.

RUTH WHITE

Belle Prater's Boy

A YEARLING BOOK

Published by
Bantam Doubleday Dell Books for Young Readers
a division of
Bantam Doubleday Dell Publishing Group, Inc.
1540 Broadway
New York, New York 10036

Reprinted by arrangement with Farrar Straus Giroux
Printed in the United States of America
September 1997 (book club edition)
10 9 8 7 6 5
OPM

for Dee Olivia

It is only with the heart that one can see rightly; what is essential is invisible to the eye.

—Antoine de Saint-Exupéry
The Little Prince

Belle Prater's Boy

One

Around 5:00 a.m. on a warm Sunday morning in October 1953, my Aunt Belle left her bed and vanished from the face of the earth.

"When I heard her get up, I figgered she was going outside to the toilet," her husband, my Uncle Everett, told the sheriff. "So I dozed off back to sleep. When I came awake again, I'd say maybe a half hour had passed, and she wadn't back, so I says to myself, 'Reckon I better go check on Belle, see if she's okay.' So I did."

Uncle Everett, a coal miner, and Aunt Belle, along with their boy, Woodrow, lived way far in the head of a long, isolated holler called Crooked Ridge, near the town of Coal Station, Virginia, where the Appalachians are steep and rugged. In those days the roads were narrow and rocky, barely passable in bad weather. They had an old Ford, and that morning it was parked on the slope with the key in the ignition like always. Their nearest neighbors, the Sloans, who lived almost a mile down the road, told the sheriff they hadn't seen or heard a thing out of the ordinary.

According to Uncle Everett, Aunt Belle was barefooted and wearing only a thin nightgown. Her two pairs of shoes and all her clothes were still in their rightful places. There was no evidence of foul play and no indication that she went traipsing off to somewheres else. Besides, there was no place to traipse unless she went over those wild hills in her night clothes, barefooted. And in that case, somebody surely would've noticed her on the other side. There were no fresh footprints anywhere, not even in that marshy place by the gate, no unusual sound heard by Uncle Everett, or Woodrow, who was sleeping in the loft.

Never before had anything like this happened in our county, and once the word got out, folks were fairly jolted out of their ruts.

"Why, whoever heard tell of a body vanishing into thin air?" they said.

"If the truth be known," some said, "there's a corpse to be found in them woods somewheres."

Others said, "There musta been somebody waiting

down the road a piece in a car, and she rode off with him."

"But folks would've seen or heard a car up the holler that morning, wouldn't they?"

"Seems like they would."

And the speculation went on.

My mama, Love Ball Dotson, speech and drama teacher at Coal Station High School and sister to the missing person, was plenty upset. In a *Mountain Echo* interview she said it wasn't bad enough having your sister disappear like that without a trace, oh no, people had to go running their mouths and making an already tragic situation worse. It was just too much, she said, too much. Granny and Grandpa Ball, Mama's and Aunt Belle's parents, wanted to take Woodrow to live with them, but Uncle Everett wouldn't hear of it.

The days and weeks passed with nothing new coming to light. When the weeks turned into months, the hill folks settled back into their humdrum lives and Belle Prater became a kind of folk heroine, like Rose Conley in the song "Down in the Willow Gardens." In fact, somebody did write a song about Aunt Belle, and it was sung in Coal Station's main honky-tonk— the Busy Bee—accompanied by a bluegrass band, but Mama double-dared anybody ever to sing it in her presence. There were insinuations in it, she said.

When Aunt Belle had been gone for six months, it

was brought to our attention that Uncle Everett was wetting his whistle to the point of saturation every chance he got.

"Not a healthy environment for a young boy," my Granny Ball declared.

So she insisted on taking Woodrow into her home, and this time there was no objection from Uncle Everett.

Coal Station—"in the heart of the coalfields," as the local radio station, WCSV, proudly proclaimed— was a dingy mountain town built at the convergence of Black River and Slag Creek. It was no more than a wide place in the road between the hills. On the town's outskirts were the work yards, where railroad cars loaded up coal from all over the county and carried it to points east and north. That's how Coal Station got its name.

Coal Station had only two streets, and they followed the lay of the land. There was Main Street, where all the businesses were located, running parallel to Black River. And there was Residence Street, the only place around for miles where you could build a house without going up in a holler or hanging it off the side of a hill. It ran parallel to Slag Creek.

Residence Street was, in fact, the brightest spot in all the county, and among the other nice houses there was the one in which I, Gypsy Arbutus Leemaster, lived with my mother and stepfather, Porter Dotson, editor of the *Mountain Echo*. Our house was a modern, one-story brick ranch, with white shutters, a front porch, and the only picture window in town. We had a telephone, two radios, a phonograph, a refrigerator, a stand-up freezer, and an electric stove. Next door to us Granny and Grandpa Ball had the same conveniences in one of those big old, white, green-shuttered, two-story houses with a wraparound porch on both floors. They also had a television set where you could sometimes see one real fuzzy channel from Charleston, West Virginia, if the weather was perfect. It was the mountains, according to Grandpa, interfering with reception. Surrounding our two houses was a wide expanse of cool green grass and about fifty apple trees which we called the orchard. What a wonder and a joy to behold in the spring when they all bloomed! There were also azaleas, pink and fuchsia. Not to mention the lilac bushes down by the creek, and the wild dogwood. People walking by our houses would sometimes stop there on the road and look and look, like they couldn't believe their dadburned eyes.

And that was the general appearance of my world that spring when Woodrow came to us—everything fresh and bright, pink and white. Mama reminded me how privileged I was, how fortunate, and I didn't doubt her word one bit, except when a certain nightmare came to haunt me. Then I couldn't help feeling more plagued than privileged. It had something to do with a dead animal, and I would wake up sobbing or screaming.

Even though Aunt Belle was Mama's sister, I had seen very little of her and Woodrow in my whole life. I had the idea from somewhere that there had been some kind of rift between the two sisters years ago, but when I asked Mama about it, she said, "Of course not! We were close. We loved each other."

Still, I wondered.

Woodrow had lived way up in the head of that holler with his mother and father without any plumbing or even a refrigerator, and he and I had always gone to different schools. We were the same age, as I had turned twelve in November and he had turned twelve sometime in January that year, and we were the same size—four feet ten inches tall and ninety-two pounds—but we had practically nothing else in common that I knew of then. Woodrow was gawky and backward and wore hillbilly clothes that were hand-me-downs from his daddy and his daddy's brother, Russell. Once, when we were about ten, I saw Woodrow, and his pants were too long and too big in the waist, so he had a rope tied around his middle to keep them up. He sure looked funny that day, and I think he felt self-conscious, too, because it was my birthday and I had on a frilly blue dress and black patent-leather slippers. Another time when I saw him at Christmas, he had on an oversized cap where you could pull the flaps down over your ears. He was proud of that ugly old thing.

And I'll tell you something else about Woodrow— though I really don't want to—he was cross-eyed. Sometimes you couldn't tell if he was looking at you or not, and he had to wear real thick glasses.

I couldn't wait to visit Woodrow that spring night when he moved in next door. I wanted to know if he had any secret knowledge or theories about what had happened to his mother.

It was a Friday, and I was in my blue jeans, parked on a stool in front of my dresser while Mama plaited my blond hair in two long pigtails, the way I liked to wear it when I had a chance to play. It was the only way I could tolerate having hair longer than Rapunzel's.

"Now, don't you go over there and aggravate him about Aunt Belle, you hear me?" Mama said to me.

"Gee whiz! I'm not a moron," I protested.

"Well, I should hope not," she said. "He's been through a lot, and he deserves some consideration. So don't go pestering him to death."

"Pester him? You make me sound like a cockroach!"

Mama giggled.

"Go on, then, and cheer him up. Tell him the eyeball joke. It's so funny, and you tell it so well."

I swelled up a bit. It was a known fact that I could tell good jokes. Mama pecked me on the cheek and we smiled at each other in the mirror. My mama was very beautiful. Everybody said so. And she smelled good all the time—like Christmas candy. And her hair put you in mind of one of those Halo shampoo ads.

I slid off the stool and headed out the door.

"Tell him hey for me, and welcome," Mama called after me.

It was a mystic twilight I found myself in that first of the many times to follow when I raced across our yards to go visit Woodrow. The apple trees sprinkled tiny petals on me. The breeze whipped them and their sweet aroma around me so that I was heady with a strange excitement as I entered the door, yelled hello to Granny and Grandpa, and galloped up the stairs to Woodrow's room at the front of the house.

His shaggy blond hair was hanging down in his eyes, and he kept tossing it to the side. He was putting his few pitiful belongings into a dresser drawer. And in the middle of the bed was Grandpa's German shepherd, who had no name but Dawg. She was sweet and everybody loved her, but if Granny saw Dawg sprawled there in the middle of the bed, she would pitch one big fit. Woodrow had some things to learn.

"Hiya, neighbor," I said, and tossed a cherry jawbreaker to Woodrow.

He caught it, then looked at that piece of candy like it was pure gold.

"Joe Palooka!" he said.

We both unwrapped our jawbreakers and popped them into our mouths. I parked on the bed and started to pet Dawg. She licked my hand, and I scratched behind her ears. Then she rolled over and stuck all her paws up in the air like she was saying, "Scratch my belly, why don'tcha?" So I scratched her belly, and one of her back legs began to jerk. The harder I scratched, the faster her leg went.

"Wanna hear a joke, Woodrow?" I said.

"Sure."

He sat down on the bed beside me and Dawg.

"There was this man, see," I said. "Went into a beer joint and said to the barkeeper, 'I bet you a free beer I can bite my own left eyeball.'

"The barkeeper just laughed and said, 'Nobody can bite his own eyeball. It's a bet.'

"So the man took out his left eyeball and bit it and popped it right back into place. It was a glass eye, see?

"Well, everybody in the joint like to died laughing, and the man drank his free beer.

"Then the same man said to the barkeeper, 'I bet you another beer I can bite my right eyeball.'

" 'What!' the barkeeper said. 'Impossible! You can't have two glass eyes! It's a bet!'

"So the man promptly took out his false teeth and bit his right eyeball with them."

That joke worked every time. I thought Woodrow would split.

While he was finishing up his belly laugh, I was trying to figure out how I was going to bring up the subject of his mother without playing the part of the cockroach. Pestering was something I didn't like to do when it could be avoided, but I told myself maybe it really couldn't be avoided. So I shrugged away all of Mama's admonitions and blurted it out.

"Now, Woodrow, about your mama. You must have some idea, some theory, about what happened to her, don'tcha?"

"Well . . ."

He wiped his nose on his shirtsleeve and didn't say anything more. I tried again.

"Grown-ups can be stupid sometimes, can't they? They overlook the most important things."

Woodrow nodded silently in agreement, but still said nothing.

"I mean, Woodrow, didn't you know something or notice something that nobody else noticed? Ain't there something you never told anybody, figgering they'd laugh at you 'cause you're a kid, you know?"

"Yeah," Woodrow said suddenly. "There was something."

He turned his crossed blue eyes on me and I nearly

swallowed my jawbreaker, because I didn't expect him to deliver so soon.

"What?" I said.

"I tried to talk to Daddy about it, but he wouldn't listen," Woodrow said.

Then he went to his chest of drawers and pulled out a book.

"I don't want anybody to know about this, Gypsy," he whispered.

"What is it?" I whispered back.

"I'll tell you if you promise to be my best friend," he said.

"I would be honored, Woodrow!" I said, genuinely pleased.

He grinned all over, showing great white teeth and a tongue stained with the cherry candy. Carefully he placed the book in my hands.

One Thousand Beautiful Poems were the words staring up at me.

"This book was a gift to Mama from Grandpa Ball when she graduated from high school," Woodrow said. "She loved it. For the last few days before she disappeared, there's a poem she read over and over. She memorized it. She clutched the book close like this . . ."

Woodrow reclaimed the book and demonstrated by holding it close to his heart.

"And she took on the most wonderful expression around her eyes, and she looked out at the hills—no, beyond the hills—beyond the earth even—and she said this poem. It's on page 88."

He handed the book to me and quickly I flipped to page 88. It read:

The breeze at dawn has secrets to tell you.
                    Don't go back to sleep.
You must ask for what you really want.
                    Don't go back to sleep.
People are going back and forth across the doorsill
                    where the two worlds touch.
The door is round and open.
                    Don't go back to sleep.

        —Jalal al-Din Rumi, thirteenth century

"What does it mean, Woodrow?" I whispered.

"Don't you see?" he said.

Then he leaned in close and ran his fingers under the words as he read.

"*The breeze at dawn has secrets to tell you,*" he read. "She knew! I know she knew something was going to happen at dawn."

"But what?" I said.

"Then it goes on to say, *Don't go back to sleep.* So she didn't. She got up and went outside."

"And what happened, Woodrow? What then?"

"I don't know," he said. "I just don't know."

"That's all?" I said, disappointed.

"Yeah," he said sadly. "That's all I know. She got up at dawn and went outside because she expected something to happen, and nobody ever saw her again."

He closed the book and clutched it to his heart.

"But it's all here," he whispered mysteriously. "The secret is hiding in the lines of this poem."

TWO

"Why did you name her Belle?" I shouted at Granny the next morning.

I shouted because she and Grandpa were both hard-of-hearing but too stubborn to wear a hearing aid. So a lot of shouting went on in that house. We didn't even notice it anymore, and everybody who came in to visit picked up the habit.

"Belle's a perfectly good name," Granny said.

We were in her big, breezy, yellow kitchen finishing up a birthday cake for my stepfather. He and Mama were gone to Abingdon to see some of Porter's kin, and Grandpa and Woodrow were out buying clothes. I sure was glad of that.

"But Belle Ball is *not* a perfectly good name," I yelled. "Didn't you know kids make fun of names like that?"

Granny placed a tiny blue rose on top of the cake.

"The idea was that she would be the belle of the ball," Granny said, and gazed out the window with a long-ago look in her eyes. "We always hoped she would be."

"And was she?" I said.

"No, dear. Your mama was the belle of *every* ball. She was near about the prettiest thing on the planet. And poor Belle . . ."

Granny sniffed a little, then abruptly came back to the present.

"There now. Soon's you put the candles on, we'll be all done. It's a right pretty cake."

"And what about poor Belle?" I said.

"Do what?"

"Aunt Belle!" I hollered. "And poor Belle what?"

Granny sighed, wiped her hands on her apron, and sat down at the table.

"She was plain, Gypsy, and that seemed to be the most important thing in the world to her—her looks. Oh, she wanted so much to be beautiful like Love.

"Your mama was—and still is—a natural beauty. She'd pop outa bed of a morning looking like the Camay soap girl. And Belle had to work hard at her looks, then still not have much to show for her efforts."

"What about boys?" I said.

Granny didn't answer, and I wondered if she had heard me.

"Boys!" I yelled. "Did Mama get all the boyfriends, too?"

Still, Granny didn't answer, and again she looked out the window, where it seemed like she could see the past shimmering on a movie screen.

"Granny?"

"I heard you. I heard you," she said at last. "I'm not hard-of-hearing, you know. I was just debating with myself whether you oughta hear this or not, but I reckon you're old enough to understand. Just don't repeat any of this to Woodrow. It would only make him sad."

"Okay," I said, propping my elbows on the table and my chin in my hands. "I wouldn't hurt Woodrow's feelings. So tell me."

"Well, Belle couldn't hold on to a boyfriend to save her soul. Every boy who walked into this house was pulled to Love like she was one powerful magnet and he was just a li'l ol' weak piece of scrap metal.

"Then Love went away to college, you know, over to Radford to learn to be a teacher like her daddy.

And for the first time Belle had boyfriends of her own. She went to dances and parties and took on a bloom in her cheeks. She was almost pretty, and having the time of her life. Then along came Amos."

"Amos!" I sputtered, as one of my elbows fell off the table. "Amos who?"

"Amos Leemaster, your daddy."

"My daddy was Aunt Belle's sweetheart first?"

"Yes, he was. Here he came riding over Cold Mountain on a black horse one Saturday in January. Big as life. I'll never forget it. Dark and rugged as the hills. Straight he was in the saddle. Nobody in Coal Station ever saw the likes of Amos Leemaster."

Suddenly, without warning, I felt hot tears well up into my eyes, and my chin started to quiver. But Granny wasn't noticing me. She was watching my daddy come riding over Cold Mountain on that long-ago Saturday.

"Said he came to open a hardware store, but he did lots more than that. He started the Civic League, you know, and their main job is distributing food to the hungry, and he also started the volunteer fire department.

"Why, he was like a knight in shining armor, and every girl in town went mental, but it was our Belle who turned his head. He was bound to marry her, he said, on that first day he hit Coal Station. They were so happy together. I never saw her sparkle like she did that spring.

"'Our Belle has found her life,' I said to your grandpa. 'She's happy now.'

"'Yeah, until Love comes home' was all he said.

"Joel could see those things coming. I never could, but I should have in this case. I guess I thought fate could not be so unkind. But it was . . ."

Granny's voice trailed away. I swallowed hard three times before I could trust my own voice again.

"And then what happened?" I asked.

"Oh, the rest is history," Granny said. "It was like fireworks, as they say in the movies, the minute Amos and Love laid eyes on each other."

We were both quiet then. I didn't want to hear any more.

"Aunt Belle," I said to her in my mind, "I wish I had known you better. And I wish I knew what happened to you."

"Did you buy Porter a birthday present, Gypsy?" Granny changed the subject.

"No, did you?"

"Don't I always? You shoulda bought him something, too."

"Why?" I snapped. "He's not my daddy."

"Hush! You devilish young'un!" Granny scolded. "No, he's not your daddy, but Amos Leemaster is dead now. Nobody can help that. You treating Porter like you do won't bring your daddy back."

"I don't treat him bad," I said, and ran my finger around the edge of the cake plate to catch the frosting drippings.

"Not as bad as I'd like to," I mumbled real low, and popped the frosting into my mouth.

"You just give him the silent treatment all the time," Granny went on as she got up and carried the dirty cake tins to the sink. "You know it hurts his feelings."

It was true. Funny thing was, I used to like Porter Dotson fine when he was just the feller down the street who ran the newspaper. He was funny and friendly. Then he married my mama two years ago, and I stopped liking him. Every time I saw him sitting there where my daddy used to sit reading the paper by the picture window, I wanted to shout at him, "Move your carcass outa my daddy's place!"

But instead, I didn't say anything at all, sometimes for days on end. Even if he asked me a point-blank question, I wouldn't answer him. Yeah, it was wicked of me. I enjoyed seeing that bewildered look come over his face. He didn't know how to react. Porter never had kids of his own, and I think he expected me to be like a puppy—you know—playful and cute and adoring. But I could tell him one thing right now—I was no puppy! And he was in for a real sorry time of it trying to be Gypsy Leemaster's stepfather.

"Here comes your grandfather and Woodrow," Granny said, looking out the window. "I best get some lunch ready."

Three

___

I ran to the front door to meet them. They were both loaded down with pokes that were crammed full, and Woodrow was so tickled he couldn't stop grinning. I knew Grandpa must have bought him lots of stuff. Dawg came bounding in behind Woodrow, barking with excitement.

"You gotta see, Gypsy!" Woodrow jabbered. "You gotta see what Grandpa bought me. I never had so much new stuff all at one time."

I helped Woodrow unload on Granny's wine-colored horsehair couch.

"Lookit the comic books!" he gushed. "Red Ryder and Lulu and Sluggo and Joe Palooka and Slime!"

"Comic books!" I said, laughing. "What about clothes? Didn't you go out to buy clothes?"

"Yeah," Woodrow said. "Them, too. Britches and shirts and socks and belts and underwear and *two* pairs of shoes, and shorts for summertime, and what else, Grandpa?"

"Eh?" Grandpa said as he dumped his sacks beside Woodrow's.

He hadn't heard a word. Woodrow went plowing through the pile of new things.

"Here it is, Gypsy! *Slime!*"

Proudly he produced a comic book with a picture of a big fat maggot on the front cover. We sprawled on one of those round braided rugs Granny always kept on her slick and shiny hardwood floors, put our heads together, and read *Slime* out loud to each other, hootin' and hollerin' at the most disgusting stories ever.

Directly Granny called from the kitchen, "All right now, you young'uns, come on in here and eat these 'tater cakes I made you."

All four of us were in high spirits as we ate lunch. We acted the fool and yelled at each other over the table so the people all up and down Residence Street could probably hear every word. All the windows and doors were wide open. Granny did make the best 'tater cakes, and Woodrow and I ate three apiece.

"Now, Woodrow," Granny said when we were done

eating, "I want you to put all your new things away in your room. Then I want you to trot down to Main Street and get a haircut. Gypsy can show you where the barbershop is."

Woodrow put his hand to his head and felt his hair.

"You want me to get my hair cut in a haircuttin' store?" he said.

That was a real knee-slapper, but Woodrow didn't seem to mind our laughing. He went right along with us. In fact, I think he was putting us on.

"You never been to a barbershop before, Woodrow?" I said.

"No. When my hair got down in my eyes, Daddy would set a bowl on top o' my head, and whatever was hanging past the rim of the bowl, he would whack it off."

That sent us into hysterics again, and Granny had to take off her glasses and wipe them on her apron.

Woodrow changed into a pair of his new pants and a shirt, and put the rest away. Grandpa gave him fifty cents and we headed to Main Street.

It was a perfect day. The hills around us were green and full and they seemed to hold our little town in a cup away from the rest of the world. All the yards on Residence Street were as neat as a freshly made bed, and there was the smell of lilacs and fruit trees blooming everywhere.

We walked past nine houses going toward Main

Street. Then there was the post office, the courthouse, and the Presbyterian church before we reached the businesses.

WE NEED YOUR HEAD IN OUR BUSINESS read the sign over Akers's Barbershop. I had not been in there since I was a real little girl and my daddy used to take me with him when he went to get his hair cut.

There were four men sitting around talking and watching Clint Akers cut Jake Stiltner's hair. I knew they were hillbillies and that two of them mined coal for a living. It seemed there was a lot of chattering and guffawing, but when we walked in, they got quiet and looked at us. Maybe they were telling dirty jokes or something. I heard a boy at school one time say that's where he heard all his dirty jokes—at the barbershop. And he knew a lot. Well, they could just hush up for a while. They knew better than to tell a dirty joke in front of Porter Dotson's stepdaughter. That was a cross I had to bear wherever I went.

Woodrow and I perched together, one on each side of a cane-bottomed chair.

"Howya doin'?" Clint said to us.

We said, "Fine."

"Clint, this is my relation," I said, "and he needs a haircut. He's got fifty cents."

"Howya doin', young feller?" Clint said to Woodrow.

Woodrow said "Fine" again.

"Gypsy," Clint went on, "is this boy from your daddy's side of the family?"

"No, Mama's," I said.

"How's that?" Clint said as he stopped his scissors in midair and gave us his undivided attention.

"How's what, Clint?" I said, knowing perfectly well what he was driving at.

"Which one of your mama's people is he?"

Woodrow and I looked at all the waiting faces. What the heck, I thought. They were bound to find out. Might as well get it over with.

"This here's Belle Prater's boy," I said.

"Is that a fact?" Clint said, his eyes as big as silver dollars. "Belle Prater's boy, huh? What's your name, boy?"

"Woodrow."

"Woodrow, huh? Yeah, that's right. I recall reading that in the *Mountain Echo*. Her boy, Woodrow, it said, was asleep when she disappeared. So that was you?"

Woodrow didn't answer and I didn't blame him. It was a dern fool question. Nobody else said anything. They just crossed their arms and legs and leaned back and stared. Clarence Sparks aimed a big splat of tobacco juice into a tin can, then continued staring with the others.

Finally Esau Ward said, "You heard anything from your mama, boy?"

"Now, Esau!" I said, more than a little aggravated.

"You know doggone good and well if there was any news about Aunt Belle, it would be all over the county. You wouldn't have to ask."

"That's the truth," Clint said, laughing; then he went back to his haircutting.

The atmosphere in the room lightened up some, and after a while a hushed conversation started again.

"Okay, Woodrow, your turn," Clint said as he took fifty cents from Jake.

"But they were here first," Woodrow said politely, motioning to the others in the room.

"Oh, them!" Clint said, laughing again. "They don't want no haircuts. They're just chewing the fat."

Woodrow took his place in the barber chair.

"Folks always come to my place to socialize," Clint went on, like he was bragging. "Why, I remember Gypsy's daddy, Amos Leemaster, used to drop by just to talk sometimes. And he'd bring Gypsy with him. You remember that, Gypsy?"

I nodded.

"I reckon Amos took Gypsy with him nearabout every place he went, didn't he, Gypsy?"

I nodded again.

"You never saw one without the other," Clint went on, determined to wear the subject out. "I never saw a man who loved his young'un more. He was the finest and handsomest man I ever seed. It was a pity what happened to him . . ."

"Don't cut too much!" Woodrow interrupted Clint suddenly, for which I was grateful.

"Well, I ain't even started yet," Clint said. "Don't worry, boy. You'll get your money's worth and no more. That's what I always tell people. You'll get your money's worth and not a lick more."

Raymond Muncy came in and took a chair by Esau and Clarence.

"Hidy, Raymond," Esau said; then he leaned over and whispered something.

They both looked at Woodrow.

"Belle Prater's boy, no foolin'? Cross-eyed, ain't he?" Raymond said.

"Was Belle cross-eyed?" Clarence asked.

"Oh no," Raymond said. "I went to school with Belle and she wadn't no beauty like Love, but she wadn't cross-eyed either."

I had had about enough of this.

"Hey, Raymond," I said as loud and nasal as I could manage, the way I had heard some of the holler women talk. "How's your girl Flo? I heard she fell off the running board and caught her foot under the wheel."

"You heard right, Gypsy," Raymond said. "But she's mending. She'll be back in school on Monday."

"Glad to hear it, Raymond. Flo's as good a girl as you'll find—right smart, too."

" 'Zat so?" Raymond said, and seemed to puff up.

"Well, sometimes I think she's the smartest one of my seven, even if she is a girl."

I thought I was the only one in the room who detected that disguised insult to the whole female gender, but no, there was Woodrow peeping around the side of his glasses at me. He never missed a thing. And it occurred to me that Woodrow would never say anything like that. He did not think of me as "just a girl" any more than I thought of him as a cross-eyed boy.

Four

"Gypsy," Granny called from the front porch as we approached the house. "Just 'cause Woodrow's here, don't think you can get out of practicing your hour like always. And don't forget you gotta unplait your hair and wash it before the party."

I groaned. It wasn't the piano practice I minded, but when it came to washing my hair, I'd rather clean up vomit. It had to be done twice a week no matter what, and it took hours to dry. If that wasn't enough, I had to brush it one hundred strokes every night to make it strong and shiny. After that Mama always rolled the ends for me on paper rollers, which I slept in. My hair was a great source of pride for her. She would tell everybody how many inches long it was and how many years *she* had been growing it, like it was one of her prize azalea bushes or something. To even hint at cutting my hair could spoil her day.

"What party?" Woodrow said. "And what are you practicing?"

"Oh, it's Porter's birthday," I said. "We always have a big supper and a cake on everybody's birthday."

"Hot dog!" Woodrow said.

"And I have to practice the piano an hour on Saturday and an hour on Sunday and a half hour on weekdays. I've been taking lessons from Granny since I was six years old. You know, she was a piano teacher for forty years, but I'm her only student now."

"How can she teach with her bad hearing?" Woodrow said.

"She watches my hands when we're having a lesson, and she can see a wrong note almost before I hit it. It seems as her hearing gets worse, her vision gets better."

As we reached the porch, Dawg greeted us. We sat down and petted her.

"You know, *she* played the piano," Woodrow said softly.

"She who?" I said.

"Mama. Granny taught her, too. She played so pretty it made me want to cry."

"Y'all didn't have a piano in that li'l ol' shack, didja?" I said, then bit my tongue. "I mean . . ."

"No," Woodrow said, seeming not to notice my blunder. "Mama always wanted one. She played over at the church on Poplar Creek of a Sunday. Can Aunt Love play?"

"No," I said. "She never could get the hang of it. Granny told me that Mama tried her best to learn, but she was so bad when she started practicing, the dogs would leave home."

We giggled.

I did my duty that afternoon, and about 7:00 p.m. we all settled down to supper in Granny's dining room.

There sat Mama looking like royalty, with Porter beside her, his arm draped across the back of her chair. Porter's brother, Hubert Dotson, the town doctor—we called him Doc Dot—was there with his wife, Irene, and two little twin girls, Dottie and DeeDee Dotson. Woodrow started giggling when he heard their names, so I whispered to him, "That's not the worst of it. Porter and Doc Dot's daddy was named Bobby Robert Dotson."

I thought Woodrow was going to have to leave the table when I said that.

"What are you two young'uns giggling about?" Grandpa said.

He was standing at the head of the table fixing to carve the pork roast. When I looked up at him with his thinning hair and wire-rimmed specs, it struck me how much he favored Harry Truman.

"Nothing," I managed to say.

"Nothing?" Porter said. "Well, nothing seems to be mighty funny."

Everybody looked at us, but nobody was mad. They were smiling and in a good mood, and glad to see Woodrow having fun.

"Well now, Mother, is that a bottle of your home-made blackberry wine I see there on the sideboard?" Porter shouted to Granny.

"Oh Lordy, yes, I nearly forgot," Granny said, and fetched the bottle to the table. "Here, Doc Dot, will you do the honors?"

She set the wine in front of him.

"Certainly," Doc Dot said as he stood up to open and serve the wine. "You know, all a body needs is a taste of spirits to soothe the nerves. Sometimes a little sip from a bottle like this one in front of me could mean the difference between sanity and insanity, and frankly . . ."

Doc Dot had a twinkle in his eye as he raised his voice for the benefit of Granny and Grandpa.

"Frankly, I'd rather have a bottle in front of me than a frontal lobotomy!"

We all just about died laughing.

Doc Dot was so tickled with his success he decided to try again.

"Speaking of tension," he said. "Mose Childress came to see me the other day and he said, 'Doc, one night I dreamed I was a tepee and the next night I dreamed I was a wigwam. What do you think my problem is?'

"And I said, 'Well, Mose, that's simple enough. Your problem is, you're just two tents!' "

That one got a good laugh, too. And so it went all evening. The wine seemed to loosen everybody up, Granny's cooking was blue ribbon, and even Porter didn't get on my nerves as much as usual. I caught myself almost smiling at him once.

"Can we do this on my birthday?" Woodrow suddenly blurted out when there was a quiet moment.

Then, seeming to regret his boldness, he ducked his head into his plate and blushed scarlet.

There came a chorus of replies:

"Certainly!"

"Of course!"

"Naturally!"

"When is your birthday, Woodrow?" I said.

"January 1," Woodrow said, smiling with pleasure at all this attention. "Or December 31. Mama never knew for sure. I was borned right on the stroke of midnight, New Year's Eve, 1942."

"Right on the stroke!" Mama said. "Belle never told us that."

"Well, she told me lots of times. She told me that story so many times I know it by heart. A midwife was with her and she was having a real hard time. She was trying and trying to birth me, but I wouldn't come. Finally Mama passed out from all the pain and she went out of her body. Then she felt peaceful and free. She said she drifted around the room and could see the midwife and her own body on the bed.

"Then she realized she wasn't alone. Another person was there floating around with her. It seemed like it was somebody who just arrived from far away, and it was somebody she felt like she used to know a thousand years ago in another place.

"And Mama said to that person, 'Oh, it's you! I've waited for you, and I missed you so much! What took you so long?'

"And the person said, 'I couldn't get away. They just now let me go. But here I am, so let's get started.'

"Then Mama came to herself and she heard the clock strike midnight, and I was borned all at the same time."

"Who do you think it was she met?" my mama said breathlessly.

I looked at her and at the others. All their eyes were on Woodrow. The wine and cake were forgotten in the fascination of his story.

"Why, it was me!" Woodrow cried joyfully. "Me!"

There was complete silence as we digested what he had said. A shiver ran up my spine as I thought what a strange story that was.

Suddenly there was a ring, and we all jumped like we were shot. Then we laughed nervously as Mama ran to answer the phone. It was for Doc Dot. Somebody was having a fit up on Grassy Lick and he had to go see about him. The party scattered when he left. The twins curled up on the couch and went to sleep while the women cleared up the dishes, and Grandpa and Porter commenced discussing President Eisenhower.

Woodrow and I went out to feed Dawg; then we sat in the swing on Granny's tremendous porch. It was a still, clear night. The moon was full and there were millions of stars. The mountains loomed over us like friendly giants, and we could hear the frogs having a spring fling down in Slag Creek.

"This is the day I will choose," Woodrow said softly.

"Choose for what?" I said, and yawned.

I was about ready to turn in.

"Mama told me when we die, we're allowed to live one day over again—just one—exactly as it was. This is the day I will choose."

I was surprised. A day that for me had been only slightly special was the most wonderful day of his life.

It made me wonder how bad things had been in Crooked Ridge.

Then we talked real serious about the pagan babies over there across the ocean dying with filth diseases. And what about those poor folks in New York City who were living practically stacked on top of one another. And in Russia they had gobs of people all living together in one little bitty house. If you complained, they had you hauled off to Siberia to live in an igloo and see how you liked that. Both of us said we felt real lucky to live right here on Residence Street.

"I wonder how my mama could ever have left here to marry my daddy and go live up there with him," Woodrow said. "It seems like this beautiful place has everything you could ever want, and nothing could ever hurt you here."

Five

Almost an hour later Mama and I were in front of the mirror in my room as she rolled my hair for the night. She was in her thin rose robe for the first time of the season, and I was wearing my summer pajamas.

My room, all ruffled and lacy, was very spacious, and as pink and white as the spring, with a canopy bed; a nightstand and a lamp beside it where I always had good books to read; my own desk; a dresser with a big brass mirror over it; a chest of drawers and a closet so full of clothes I couldn't keep track of them.

"You never told me my daddy was Aunt Belle's sweetheart first," I said to Mama.

She was startled.

"Who told you that?" she said sharply.

I shrugged. "Does it matter who told me? Is it true?"

She didn't answer. She wasn't listening. Her face had taken on that hurt look I recognized as belonging to her grief for Daddy.

"I guess Aunt Belle really loved him too, huh?" I said softly.

"Love?" Mama said. "Belle was eighteen, I was nineteen, Amos was twenty-five. We were mesmerized, brainwashed, hypnotized, whatever you want to call it."

"What do you mean?"

"Oh, I don't know, my Gypsy girl," she said, and gave me a quick hug. "I guess I mean when folks are in love they say and do things they wouldn't dream of doing when they're in their right minds."

"And I guess Aunt Belle was pretty shook up when Daddy picked you over her, huh?"

"I guess so," Mama said with a sigh. "And I was so caught up in your father's spell, I'm afraid I ignored her feelings. Amos did, too. We didn't see anybody or anything but each other."

"So how did Aunt Belle take it?"

"Badly," Mama said. "She . . ."

Mama paused and I saw her chin quiver.

"She . . . she was like a whipped dog. She shut

herself up in her room, wouldn't talk to anybody, lost weight, cried . . ."

Mama abruptly walked to the window and placed her forehead gently against the frame.

"That's okay, Mama," I said quickly. "You don't have to talk about it. I was just curious, but that's okay."

She gave me a brief wave of the hand, as if to say, "I'll be all right in a minute."

So I watched her and waited. A soft, scented breeze ruffled her hair and her thin robe. She shivered and hugged herself, then walked back to me and calmly started rolling my hair again. There were tears on her cheeks.

"In the last months I have relived those days over and over again," Mama said. "And I have promised my sister in my heart that if I ever see her again, I will tell her how truly sorry I am that I caused her pain."

"But, Mama, if Daddy loved you best, that wasn't your fault. What were you supposed to do?" I said, trying to comfort her.

"I could have been kinder," Mama said.

Our eyes met in the mirror, and she smiled a sad kind of smile.

"It wasn't your fault," I insisted. "Nor Daddy's either."

"I remember that Saturday so vividly," Mama said. "The day Belle finally came out of her room. She came down the stairs all dressed up fit to kill in a red dress and bright red lipstick, and smelling like she fell in a vat of perfume. Mother and I were in the living room altering a dress I was going to wear on a date with Amos later that night.

" 'Where are you going?' I said to Belle.

"And she laughed. There was something unnatural about that laugh. I should have been more tuned in to her feelings.

"She had one of those sheer white scarves she kept twirling around her neck and through her fingers like she couldn't be still.

" 'Going to find myself a beau,' she said, and laughed again.

" 'Oh no, Belle, don't go out tonight,' Mother pleaded with her. 'It's payday for the miners and the town is full of drunks.'

"But she was out the door in a flash. We should have stopped her right then. We should have sat down with her and talked to her. We should have seen how alone she felt. But we didn't.

"And that was the night she met Everett Prater. She ran off with him and sent us word the next day she was okay. A week later she sent word again she was married. And two weeks later she came home and got all her stuff while we were gone to church.

"We were shocked at her behavior. Don't get me wrong. Everett's okay. A bit dull, maybe, but a good man, I guess. It's just the way she did it, you know, picking up the first man that showed an interest in her. I guess she was lucky it was Everett. She could have done worse.

"At the time it seemed to me a terribly immature, impulsive, reckless thing she did, and so spiteful! Like she hated us. Like it didn't matter who she married as long as she got away from us.

"But now I see it with different eyes. She was so hurt . . . and desperate. She had to leave, not because she hated us, but because seeing me and Amos together every day was like opening up a wound over and over."

Mama walked back to the window.

"Now I almost admire her for what she did then," Mama said, more to the night than to me. "She was courageous in an odd sort of way. It was like stepping off a familiar and safe place into darkness, not knowing . . ."

"Maybe she's done it again," I interrupted. "Have you ever thought of that, Mama?"

Slowly she turned back to me.

"Yes, I have thought of that. But there's Woodrow. I don't think she would leave him on purpose."

I crawled into bed and Mama tucked me in.

"How grown-up you seem tonight, Gypsy," she said wistfully. "It's almost like talking to another adult."

"Really?" I said, pleased.

"Really. But now give me some little-girl sugar and get some shut-eye."

I slept in the soft night with the sounds and smells of spring in my senses, and my dreams were filled with the face of my Aunt Belle. I followed her down through the corridors of bright seasons when she and Mama were girls, through warm summer nights and cold white Christmases, through schoolrooms and parties and autumn in the golden hills she climbed.

Where did you get lost, Aunt Belle?

It was near dawn that the nightmare came. Just like the ones before it, there was an animal, limp and lifeless, in a puddle of blood. Was it a deer? A dog? A kitten? An ugly, ugly thing was in that animal's face. The ugly thing that I could not see. The ugly thing . . .

I woke up crying for my mother, and I didn't feel grown-up at all, nor did I want to be. She came to me as she always did, gentle and silent, rocking me like a baby in her arms.

"I can't see its face, Mama," I sobbed. "Why can't I make out its face?"

She said nothing, but the sadness in her eyes told me she knew the answers and could not bear to tell me.

Six

"Oh, Gypsy, you're so awfully beautiful!"

These were Woodrow's words the next morning when he first saw me all dressed up for Sunday school. He was on Granny's front porch, reading the Sunday paper, which he dropped when he saw me coming.

I couldn't help smiling.

I was wearing one of those little bitty pieces of a hat with a veil barely covering my eyes. It was pink like my new dress, which had long, tapered sleeves and kick pleats on each side. I also had on pink shoes with an inch-high heel, and naturally I was wearing the white gloves every well-brought-up girl wore to church.

"You're not so bad yourself, cousin!" I said, as I looked him up and down.

He was wearing a pair of new pants and a nice blue dress shirt with a tie to match.

"I never wore one of these before," he said as he fingered the tie. "But it's kinda nice. Grandpa tied it for me."

"Ready to go?" I said.

Together we strutted down the street.

There was a Methodist and a Baptist church on up Slag Creek, and all kinds of offspring churches in the hollers, but everybody in Coal Station who was anybody a'tall, as Mama put it, went to the Presbyterian church. It was the biggest and the best. It had a tall steeple with a bell in it that rang at 11:00 on Sunday mornings and on special occasions. You could hear it echoing through the hills for miles around, and you could imagine folks stopping whatever they were doing to listen.

My Sunday-school class had about ten kids in it, ages eleven and twelve, which meant we were the in-betweens, feeling like we didn't belong anywhere—not with the teenagers, and certainly not with the young'uns.

Some, like Buzz Osborne, had had a growing spurt that shot them a head taller than the others. Some, like Willy and Mary Lee, were pure tee runts. Then there were the average ones like me and Woodrow.

But none were stingy with the questions and Woodrow got the works. Everybody talked at once.

"You live with the Balls? Since when?"

"How old are you?"

"Can you look in two directions at once?"

"You don't favor Gypsy a bit."

"How much did that tie cost?"

"Do you believe in God?"

To the last question Woodrow replied, "Yeah, I met him once."

"You met God?" they all said. "No, you didn't!"

"Yeah, I did. And you know what? He sneezed, and I didn't know what to say."

They didn't get it. Woodrow tried again.

"His name is Howard, you know."

"God's name ain't Howard!"

"Sure it is," said Woodrow. "It says so in the Lord's Prayer—'Howard be thy name.'"

That one they got.

Nobody asked Woodrow anything about Aunt Belle, and I figured they didn't get the connection. When our teacher, Mrs. Compton, came in, I introduced her to Woodrow, and she made him feel welcome, but she didn't ask him any questions at all. She went right into the lesson.

That Sunday the Presbyterian literature for intermediates dealt with Jesus healing the sick. We read

about it in the New Testament. Then we talked about
it.

"You know, boys and girls," Mrs. Compton said very
sweetly, "sickness is a bad thing, but all of us get sick
once in a while. Sometimes it's so bad we think we
are going to die. Have you ever known anyone who
was *very very* sick?"

About four people raised their hands, including
Woodrow, but I couldn't think of any sick people.

"Would one person like to tell us about someone
who was *very very* sick?" Mrs. Compton said.

Only one person raised his hand then, and that was
Woodrow.

"All right. Is it Woodrow?" Mrs. Compton said.

"Yes, ma'am," he said politely.

"Would you like to come up here, Woodrow?"

Woodrow went to the front of the class. I was
amazed. Every bright and shiny face was turned to
him, curious to hear what this new boy had to say.

"This is a story about Buck Coleman," Woodrow
began, "who had a sickness so bad . . . well . . . let
me tell you it was bad. His belly kept getting bigger
and bigger and bigger. It got big as a watermelon, but
the rest of him kept falling off. Buck finally had to go
to the doctor's, and the doctor said, 'Buck, you got
the biggest tapeworm I ever did even hear tell of, and
it's curled up in your belly getting all your food.'

"Well, the doctors tried to kill that tapeworm, but they couldn't do it without killing Buck with it. He kept eating a lot, but he was still starving to death. And, oh yeah, I forgot to tell you, he craved molasses."

Woodrow paused to let everything sink in.

"Molasses?" little Willy Stacy said.

"Yeah, molasses," Woodrow continued. "Finally the doctor decided to lure the tapeworm out."

"How was he going to lure it out?" Mary Lee Rowe said.

"With molasses, naturally. They took a big jar of molasses and held it in front of Buck's face, and the tapeworm smelled it and came crawling out to get it."

"And Buck was saved?" from Willy again.

"No, that tapeworm was so long and fat, Buck suffocated to death before it got out."

Woodrow sat down.

I thought Mrs. Compton was going to faint.

"Really, Woodrow!" she said irritably. "Was that necessary? Did that happen or did you make it up?"

"He made it up!" Buzz Osborne chimed in.

" 'Pon my word of honor," Woodrow said. "Buck Coleman was my daddy's sister's husband's uncle's cousin."

"That doesn't make it true!" Mrs. Compton shot back.

"I know a story, too," Mary Lee said. "About my

aunt who went to New York City and they fed her snails."

"Never mind!" Mrs. Compton said. "Let's talk about something else. The thought for the week is on page 36."

While everybody was turning to page 36, Woodrow glanced at me and winked so quick I don't think anybody else saw him. I ducked my head to hide the smile that had to come. That's when I knew for sure that Woodrow wasn't as backward as he let on, but he had a bit of the devil in him.

After Sunday school the church bells rang and we went out into the bright morning to listen. I thought I never had seen such a blue and green and golden day. Mama and Porter were in the choir room fixing to sing during the service, but Grandpa and Granny were outside chattering with their neighbors.

Mr. Cooper, the school principal, was okay, but he was married to a killjoy. She could hardly stand to see folks enjoying life, especially kids. It got on her nerves so bad, I was sure she lay awake nights thinking up ways to put a stop to it. And that's how it was that morning as we stood there listening to the bells and taking in the sweetness of the moment.

Suddenly she walked right up to Woodrow and grabbed him hard under the chin, lifting his face exactly like he was a horse she was looking over and fixing to buy.

"Not much for looks, is he?" she said. "Takes after his mama."

Woodrow jerked away from her with fury in his eyes, but he didn't say a word to her.

"Well now, I hope you aren't as hardheaded as she was!" Mrs. Cooper went on, placing her hands on her ample hips.

I grabbed Woodrow's arm quick and pulled him toward Granny and Grandpa.

"Grandpa, don't you have a quarter for Woodrow to put in the collection plate?" I said as loud as I could to drown out Mrs. Cooper, who was still talking.

Grandpa did have a quarter for Woodrow, and I could tell by the way he looked at that quarter Woodrow wanted to keep it for his own self, but he didn't. In fact, he made it clatter when he tossed it in the plate, so everybody would hear it.

Going back home from church, Woodrow and I skipped along in front of the family, singing. He knew all the words to "Aba Daba Honeymoon," which he taught to me.

Later we vacuumed Dawg while Granny and Mama fixed fried chicken and gravy for dinner. Granny had one of those newfangled vacuum cleaners that was so mighty it could pick up a steel ball. In fact, that's how the salesman sold it to Granny. Grandpa always teased her about it, 'cause he said if anybody had any steel balls to vacuum up, Granny's machine was ready. It was strange how Dawg wasn't one bit afraid of that vacuum cleaner, even with all the racket it made. When you went to turn it on, she would lie down in front of you and put all her legs up in the air and grin at you. That meant she was ready for a good vacuuming. So I would put on one of those attachments that was made for doing the couch and curtains, and vacuum Dawg's belly with it. She just loved it. Her four legs would paw the air at about ninety miles an hour. Woodrow got such a kick out of that, I offered to let him do the rest of Dawg, which he did, giggling all the time.

Late that evening, Woodrow and I went out to my tree house overlooking Slag Creek, which my daddy built for me when I was only five. It was a two-story job, the lower floor being the porch and the upper floor the house. Woodrow was impressed. After inspecting it throughout, he suggested we make it our secret hideout. The house part was tucked up among the leaves and blossoms so that from the ground nobody could see it unless they got up close.

"We'll put a sign on it—KEEP OUT!" Woodrow said. "And we'll stash our treasures inside."

"What treasures?" I said.

"Oh, money and stuff. We'll get some treasures."

"Treasures" was a good word. It sparked my imagination and conjured up images of kidnapped princesses and pirates and swashbuckling heroes.

"I have an old jewelry chest I don't use!" I said. "We'll bring it up here for our treasures."

We settled down on the tree-house porch and let our legs dangle out over the creek. The frogs were starting up with their party again, and all mingled in with the night sounds were the mamas calling their children to come in because tomorrow was a school day.

"Peggy Sue!"

"Franklin Delanooooo!"

"You must ask for what you really want," Woodrow said softly. "That's what Mama's poem said. And Preacher Yates said the same thing today in his sermon. Ask and you shall receive."

"What do you really want, Woodrow?"

"You won't make fun of me?"

"Oh no, Woodrow, I would never make fun of you." He smiled.

"Well, besides wanting Mama to come home safe and sound, I want my eyes to be straight," he said. "If my eyes were corrected, Gypsy, they would look just like yours."

My heart filled with pity for him, but I didn't say anything.

"What do you really want, Gypsy?"

"Oh, it sounds silly next to what you want, Woodrow. You want important things."

"But what you want is important to you no matter

how it seems to someone else. What do you really want, Gypsy?"

"I have never let those words cross my lips about the thing I really want. Mama would just about die if she heard it. And it's no use asking for what you can't have. I want to get my hair cut off short."

"But why? It's so beautiful! Nobody has hair like yours, Gypsy."

"That's for sure. And you wanna know why you don't see other people running around with their hair down to their butt? Because it's so much work! That's all I do is take care of my hair! It's disgusting."

"Oh," Woodrow said.

"But that's not all," I continued. "Sometimes . . . sometimes, Woodrow, I feel invisible. Like maybe under all this hair nobody can see me. They talk about my hair, but do they ever see what's underneath? You know what I mean?"

"No . . . not exactly," Woodrow said.

"Sometimes I want to say, 'There is a person in here!,' but it sounds silly, even to me."

Woodrow didn't say anything, and I let out a long sigh. I guess I just didn't have the right words to explain.

The night air was turning chilly. We watched the moon and listened to the mamas.

"Garnet! Am I gonna have to come out there and get you?"

"Willy! Don't you make me call you again!"

"Woodrow, do you think Aunt Belle asked for what she really wanted that morning, like the poem said?"

"Yeah, and she got it, too," he whispered.

"What? What do you mean? What did she ask for?" I said breathlessly.

"To get out of her life."

"Oh, Woodrow, you mean . . . you think she's . . ." I couldn't say the word.

"Dead? No, she ain't dead," Woodrow said matter-of-factly. "But by now she may wish she was."

"What! What do you know, Woodrow?"

"GYP . . . SY!"

It was Mama calling me.

"Nothing for sure and certain," Woodrow said.

"Gypsy, you come in now. Time to brush your hair."

I groaned.

"COM . . . ING!" I yelled back.

"I'll tell you all I know tomorrow," Woodrow said. "But you won't believe me."

"No, now! I wanna know now!"

"Not now. You gotta go brush your hair."

That was definitely the wrong thing to say to me at that particular moment, and I guess Woodrow realized his mistake too late.

"Sorry," he mumbled.

I folded my arms in stubborn resolution.

"I am not moving from this spot till you answer me.

I'll stay right here all night if I have to, or until Mama drags me outa this tree kicking and screaming."

Woodrow sighed.

"Okay," he said. "You go on home and do your stuff and go to bed. Then you get up and sneak out the window and meet me back down here."

"No foolin'?" I said, grinning.

I was excited. Never in a hundred million years would it have occurred to me on my own to do such a naughty thing.

"No foolin'," Woodrow said. "Think you can get away?"

"Oh sure," I said. "Mama and Porter will turn in about an hour from now."

"Okay, an hour, then."

So I ran home.

Seven

"There's this place, see." Woodrow began his story in a very soft voice. "Up there in Crooked Ridge, right behind our house—or shack, as you called it."

I hung my head in shame. "Oh, Woodrow, that was real hateful of me to say that."

"It don't matter. It *is* a shack," Woodrow said.

We were wrapped in blankets and sitting face-to-face, Indian-fashion, on the porch of the tree house. My hair was in curlers and we were both in our pajamas.

"Anyway, behind the shack there's a place . . . I don't rightly know how to say it . . . but the air is thick and it vibrates. You hit this warm spot and you feel the air quivering and you hear noises."

"What kind of noises?"

"Voices. Only they're funny voices. Have you ever sung a song or said words into a fan when it's running?"

"A fan? A 'lectric fan? No, can't say as I ever spoke to one."

We both giggled. How thrilling it was to be out here in the cool night tucked up among the leaves like a couple of cattypillars.

"Well, anyhow," he went on. "My Aunt Millie and me played a game with her electric fan. I would say words into it and she would try to make out what I was saying. Then she would say words . . . Get it?"

"Yeah."

"It's the rotating blades. They take the sound waves and chop them up, and it makes your voice sound real funny. I'll show you the next time we're around a fan that's running. And that's what this place sounds like."

"But I don't get it, Woodrow. It's just a place in the air?"

"Yeah, I felt it the first time when I was a kid. And it scared me real bad. I thought there was something there . . . something that wanted to get me. You know how little kids think? I would run into it sometimes when I was playing, and . . ."

"What was there to run into?"

"I don't know, Gypsy, but something was there. And you know, when I would try to find it—that's when I wasn't afraid of it anymore—I would walk back and forth and stop here and bend there and stretch around, but I couldn't find it when I was looking for it.

"But when I had my mind on something else, and I was just walking by or turning or doing something ordinary, boom! There it was!"

"There what was?"

"That's what I'm trying to tell you. It was just a place in the air where . . ."

"Where what?"

"Where two worlds touch," he said, and let his breath out with the words.

"That's what the poem says," I whispered.

"Yeah," Woodrow said. *"People are going back and forth across the doorsill / where the two worlds touch. / The door is round and open."*

I was lost, but I didn't want Woodrow to see how confused I was, so I kept my mouth shut.

"Mama knew about the place," Woodrow went on. "We used to talk about it sometimes; then suddenly one day she told me to hush up about that place. She didn't want me to talk about it anymore. She said I was imagining things, but even after that, I saw her out there sometimes going around and around and back and forth, kinda batting at the air like she was feeling for it."

We were quiet for a long time, and a suspicion started worming its way into my head—that Woodrow was pulling my leg.

"And for the last few days before she disappeared, whenever Daddy wasn't around, she practically lived near that spot."

"Did Uncle Everett know about that place?" I asked.

"I doubt it. I tried to tell him about it after Mama left, and he told me to hold my tongue. He said if folks heard me carrying on about a place in the air, they'd think I was addled in the head. So if he ever felt anything there or heard them voices, he kept it to his own self."

"What did the voices say, Woodrow?"

"The sound vibrated so you couldn't understand any words."

"Could you see anything there?"

"Sometimes I thought I did . . . It was like a shadow, then a flicker, real quick. I don't know. It's real hard to explain."

"Woodrow, are you teasing me?"

"*No!*" he insisted as he shook his head from side to side. "Now I may tease a Sunday-school class, Gypsy—which I did—but I would never tease you. It's true."

Suddenly from the street a mellow voice could be heard singing as it cut through the sounds of spring.

He was some mother's darling,
Some mother's son.
Once he was fair
And once he was young.

"What is that?" Woodrow said as he scooted closer to me.

"What? Oh, that singing? That's just old Blind Benny."

"Who's Blind Benny?" he said.

"He's a man who hangs out at night. He walks the streets and sings and goes through folks' trash and talks to the dogs. They love him and follow him around."

"He can sing good," Woodrow said. "Is he really blind?"

"Yeah. Doc Dot told me he practically has no eyes at all. And that makes him look like something from a horror comic, you know? Folks used to be scared of him, but he wouldn't hurt a body as far as I know. Some folks poked fun at him and said nasty things. Then he quit coming out in the daylight. He sleeps in the day and comes out at night, when there's nobody to look at him."

"Where does he live?"

"I don't know. When it gets daylight, he vanishes, and you don't see him again till dark."

"Just like a bat," Woodrow said.

"Tell me more about that hole in the air," I said.

"It's not a hole."

"Then what is it?"

"I told you, I believe it's where two worlds touch."

"So what's it got to do with Aunt Belle?"

"I think she went across the doorsill."

I was getting cranky.

"Woodrow!"

"I told you you wouldn't believe me."

"Well, you've got to admit it's not an easy story to swallow, now, is it?" I said.

"Maybe not, but it's what I believe," he said.

"Did she do it on purpose?" I asked.

"She read me this book," Woodrow said. "It was called *The Twenty-fifth Man*. It was about a man called Ed Morrell who was in prison. In fact, he was in Alcatraz, and he would get in trouble with the guards all the time. They didn't like him a bit, because he was smart. But anyhow, whenever he got in trouble, they put him in a straitjacket, and it would be so tight he couldn't even move a muscle. It was the most awfulest thing you could do to a man, and some men died in

that straitjacket, because it squeezed the life right out
of their body.

"So one day Mama was reading out loud to me
about that straitjacket, and suddenly she stopped reading and said, 'I know how he feels. I am in a straitjacket,
too. That's how I feel. Squeezed to death. I can't
move. I can't breathe. I have to get out of here.'"

Woodrow was quiet for a minute. We could hear
a night owl. I wondered what time it was getting
to be.

"Do you know what Ed Morrell did, Gypsy?" he said
softly.

"No, what?" I said.

"He would leave his body. It was the only way he
could survive. He would leave his body and go trav-
eling. He said it was the most wonderful feeling. He
would just soar away over the water and the land. He
would go see people outside the prison. Then when
the guards came to take him out of the straitjacket,
he would have to go back into his body and he didn't
want to."

"That's a good story, Woodrow."

"It's a true story. He finally got out of jail, and he
wrote the book and he went around telling people
that he had visited them when he was in the straitjacket and he would tell them what they were doing.
Folks were amazed, but they had to believe him."

"But, Woodrow, if your mama was doing that, her

body would still be somewhere, wouldn't it? I mean, that man's body was still in jail, wasn't it?"

"Yeah, Gypsy. I was just telling you Mama said she knew how he felt, how he had to get out of that strait-jacket or die. That's how Mama felt about her life. I think she kinda willed herself to leave it."

"But what about you, Woodrow?" I said. "Didn't she think about you?"

Woodrow didn't say anything.

"She was your mama," I said. "I know you miss her."

"Yeah."

> *Mary, she rocked him*
> *Her baby to sleep.*
> *Then they left him to die*
> *Like a tramp on the street.*

It was the end of Benny's song. We looked out toward the road, but we couldn't see anything except the moon shining on the apple blossoms. We could hear Blind Benny muttering cheerfully to the dogs. Dawg, freshly vacuumed, was probably among them.

We eased down the ladder and headed home.

"One last thing," Woodrow whispered before we went in opposite directions.

"What's that?" I said.

"I get a feeling sometimes," he said, "that Mama is trying to contact me."

"What makes you think that?"

"It's just a feeling. I wake up some nights and remember her voice from a dream. She's saying my name over and over . . . and she's crying. She's afraid."

I didn't know what to say.

"And her voice," he went on. "Her voice quivers like the voices in that place. She's *in* that place. I know she is."

We said good night, and I hurried across the yard and around the back of my house, shivering. I had almost reached my window when I heard a sound in the shadows.

"Gotta light?" someone said.

I like to jumped out of my skin.

A body stepped forward into the moonlight. It was Porter standing there in his pajamas, holding a cigarette.

"She won't let me smoke, you know," he said. "So I have to sneak out here after she goes to sleep . . . just like you. But I forgot my lighter."

We stood there looking at each other in the moonlight. I guess he was waiting for me to explain the situation, but it seemed like I plum forgot how to talk.

"I don't suppose you want to tell me where you've been?" he said at last.

I was trying to think, but absolutely nothing came to mind.

"No, I reckon not," he said when I didn't answer. "But I'll tell you what, you sneak in and toss me a match out the window and I'll forget I ever saw you, okay?"

I nodded, went to my window, climbed in, and pulled the blanket after me. Then I tiptoed to the dark living room, took a match from the wood box by the hearth, and hurried back to my window, where he was waiting. I handed the match to him.

"Thanks," he mumbled, and disappeared into the orchard.

I replaced the screen in my window and slipped between my sheets. Well, I was thinking, quite an ending to quite a day!

Blind Benny was coming back down the street singing:

> On the wings of a snow-white dove
> He sends his pure, sweet love

Though I had heard him sing a thousand times or more, that night I really listened to him. Yes, it was a good, strong, clear voice. It had put me to sleep many, many nights, and I had never paid attention. It had become as much a part of the mild nights as the frogs down in Slag Creek. I snuggled into my

feather bed, feeling warm and secure, and thinking
Woodrow was making me see things in a new light.

> *A sign from above*
> *On the wings of a dove.*

The ugly thing did not visit me that night.

Eight

Coal Station Elementary and Coal Station High School were both located a little piece up Slag Creek at the end of Residence Street, just before the road started getting narrow and wound on up Cold Mountain toward Kentucky.

Woodrow entered the elementary school with me the next day, and it was an experience that beat going to the fair. First of all, they put him in my room, which was Miss Hart's 6-B, one of the better places to be if you really wanted to learn, which we did. Then kids started peeking in to see him. His fame had preceded him, as the old saying goes. The tapeworm story had gone through about fifty revisions.

Even some of the uppity eighth- and ninth-graders trotted over from the high school to catch a glimpse of him. Of course, part of all this curiosity was on account of his being Belle Prater's boy, but Woodrow set everybody straight the first time her name was brought up.

"I don't know what happened to her, and I don't want to talk about it!"

He said it loud and clear so there was no misunderstanding his meaning. It made me a little ashamed of myself that I had attacked him with that question on his first night even though Mama had told me not to. But he had been real patient with me.

Anyway, the curious noses stopped twitching for the time being, so we could move on to other business. Woodrow was friendly with everybody, but especially so to Rita Presley, who was fat and always got picked on. He smiled at her and told her she had pretty hair, which she did, and then when somebody teased her, Woodrow said that was about the rudest thing he ever did hear tell of. I was proud of him, because I always had felt sorry for Rita but I never had the nerve to stand up for her like he did.

During science class that morning we talked about caves, and Woodrow made a favorable impression on Miss Hart. How he did it was first-class clever. He merely pointed out in his bashful voice—so as not to appear too know-it-all—that the way you could remember the difference between the upper and lower calcium deposits in a cave was that a stalagmite with a *g* formed from the ground, while a stalactite with a *c* formed from the ceiling.

Miss Hart was so pleased with his little lesson, I thought for a minute she was going to hug him, which would have been embarrassing, but she didn't. She grinned instead.

Woodrow was encouraged and asked if he could tell a story about a cave.

"Oh yes, please do," Miss Hart said.

Whereupon she sat down, and once again Woodrow was at the front of the class.

Woodrow's story was about Floyd Collins, a man who liked to explore the great Mammoth Cave of Kentucky. And what happened to him when he went spelunking alone one day was a sorrowful thing. He got stuck in a crevice, where he died because rescue workers could not reach him. I nearly wanted to cry when Woodrow was finished, for it was a true story.

So we went to our arithmetic lesson in a mood of seriousness. Our minds tended to hark back to that cave in Kentucky where poor Floyd suffered so awfully for weeks preceding his death. But once again it was Woodrow who saved the day.

"A puzzle! A puzzle!" The word was whispered around the room. "Woodrow has an arithmetic puzzle."

Miss Hart was smiling again.

"There were three men, see?" Woodrow began. "Went to a hotel in New York City, where I hear tell everything costs more than anywheres else. Anyway, they were charged thirty dollars just to sleep one night in a hotel room, if you can believe it. They grumbled, but each man paid his ten dollars, which makes thirty dollars, right? Then they went up the stair steps to their room, which, by the way, had three beds in it, so nobody had to double up. It wadn't no sleazy place.

"After they went up, the hotel manager suffered a 'cute attack of conscience, and he thought, well, maybe he might have overcharged the men. So he took five one-dollar bills out of his money box there under the counter, and he told the boy he had to run errands for him to take the bills up and refund the gentlemen some of their money.

"So the boy goes, and on the way he puzzles over how he can divide the five ones evenly amongst three men, and he sees no way to do it. So what did he do? He stuck two of them ones in his own pocket. Then he gave each of the three men one dollar apiece.

"Now, if you're following me, that means each man paid nine dollars for his room, right? That's twenty-seven dollars. The boy had two dollars in his own pocket, right? That's twenty-nine dollars. So what happened to the other dollar?"

Woodrow sat down. We scratched our heads. We

started scribbling and figuring. Miss Hart was calcu-
lating mentally on the ceiling. Woodrow then ad-
mitted he didn't have the answer. There was no
satisfactory answer.

Next thing we knew, it was lunchtime and it
seemed like we had just got to school. Rain poured
down and we couldn't go outside to play. So we sat
around in the classroom whispering and playing
games—hangman and tic-tac-toe.

Then somebody said, "Woodrow, do you know any
more puzzles?"

Naturally he did, sort of.

He went to the blackboard and printed in large
letters.

> C M PUPPIES?
> M R NO PUPPIES!
> O S M R PUPPIES,
> C M P N?
> L I B!
> M R PUPPIES

Once again we were stumped, until Woodrow gave us
the first line, which was, "See them puppies?"

Miss Hart couldn't keep the lid on for the rest of
the afternoon. She said it was like trying to hold thirty
corks underwater at the same time.

As for me, I never had a better school day. I told

Woodrow that very thing as we walked home at 3:30.

"Can't you hear your calling, Woodrow?" I teased him. "You're a natural-born teacher. You make learning fun."

"Oh no," Woodrow said. "I'm going to make picture shows when I grow up. My first one will be about plants that eat people. Besides, those were all Mama's stories, even the men-in-the-hotel one and the puppies one. Now, the Floyd Collins story is true, and she used to talk about it when she was blue. She said she knew exactly how Floyd Collins felt, trapped like he was in Mammoth Cave, just like Ed Morrell felt in the straitjacket . . . and just like Belle Prater felt on Crooked Ridge."

Once again we had come full circle back to his mama. And I knew it was a thing that gnawed at him all the time, and wormed its way into everything he said and did.

Granny's phone started ringing off its cradle that evening—always for Woodrow—and it didn't slow down for as long as he lived there. Which proved to me that my cousin was the most popular feller since the country singer Little Jimmy Dickens.

Nine

Friday evening, right after supper, Woodrow and I, along with Granny and Grandpa, were watching *I Led Three Lives* on television. Grandpa had to keep jumping up to adjust the horizontal hold, because the picture was flipping and rolling, and there was some snow on the screen. Other than that, you could make out people's faces for a change, and I could tell what Richard Carlson really looked like. I commented that he was right nice-looking.

"Huh!" Woodrow snorted. "I bet if a feller had *his* money, even the ugliest person could be good-looking!"

"How can money make you good-looking?" I said.

"You never heard tell of operations people get on their faces?" he said. "It costs lots of money. That's why all the movie stars look so good. Did you ever see an ugly movie star? No, you didn't. They have money. And I bet if the truth was known, a bunch of 'em were borned uglier than a mud fence."

We were stretched out on our bellies on Granny's braided rug, a box of Cracker Jacks between us. Woodrow had found the prize—a rubber ring—and I let him keep it even though it was pink and should have been for a girl.

That show ended and Dinah Shore came on singing, "See the U.S.A. in your Chevrolet! America's the greatest land of all!" And throwing us a kiss.

Dawg could be heard barking outside, and at the same time there was a knock on the front door. Woodrow and I scrambled to our feet. He beat me to the door. It was Uncle Everett.

"Howdy, son," he said quietly.

He was tall and shaggy-looking. He was wearing overalls, and in his hands was an old beat-up hat, which he twisted around and around like he was nervous.

"Howdy, Daddy! Come in!" Woodrow said, and I could tell he was tickled, but they didn't hug or even shake hands.

Woodrow held the door open for his daddy, and

Uncle Everett stepped inside. He nodded to the rest of us.

"Howdy-do," he said.

Granny and Grandpa stood up and greeted Uncle Everett and offered him a seat, which he took. At least he took the edge of it, where he perched, and didn't appear any too comfortable. I could barely remember him being in this room once . . . maybe twice before, and it occurred to me for the first time that it could be Uncle Everett felt self-conscious with us, just like Woodrow had felt that day in his oversized pants with the rope holding them up, and me in my frilly dress.

"Just wanted to check in on you, boy," Uncle Everett said. "See you're doin' okay."

"Doin' fine," Woodrow said, and parked on the floor beside his daddy's chair.

I eased down there beside Woodrow.

"You started school here, I reckon?" Uncle Everett said to him.

"Yeah, and they put me in Miss Hart's room," Woodrow said, "with Gypsy."

Uncle Everett glanced at me and nodded.

"How ya doin', Gypsy?"

"I'm fine. How's things with you, Uncle Everett?"

"I'm getting by. Yeah, I reckon I am." He said it like he wasn't too sure.

There was a moment of uncomfortable silence.

"How's Daisy and Milkweed?" Woodrow said.

"They're fine, too. No, I take that back. Daisy's fine. Milkweed busted her right front hoof on a mattock. But she's mending."

"Oh," Woodrow said. "Was she bad hurt?"

"Nah, not bad."

Another silence.

"And I guess . . ." Woodrow began, then thought better of it. "Oh, nothing."

"I don't know a bit more about her now than I knew when you left, Woodrow," Uncle Everett assured him. "But I'll be bound to come and give you any news I learn straightaway. I trust you'll do the same?"

Woodrow nodded.

"You needin' anything?" Uncle Everett asked.

"No, I got more'n I need," Woodrow said.

"Well, that's a blessing, son," Uncle Everett said. " 'Cause I'm broke as the Ten Commandments."

Then they went on with more small talk like that before Uncle Everett stood up and eased out the door. Woodrow went to the window and watched his daddy go out the walkway to the road, where the old Ford was parked. I walked over and stood at Woodrow's elbow. It was still light enough out there that I could see somebody in Uncle Everett's car. It was a blond-headed woman. Woodrow clutched the windowsill with one hand, and I could see his knuckles turning white. I didn't say a word about who that might be in Uncle Everett's car, and Woodrow didn't say anything the rest of the evening.

Ten

Granny, Grandpa, and Mama got their heads together and came to a decision about mine and Woodrow's habit of running to every picture show that came to town. I thought the new law was dumb. It said children should spend as much time as possible in the fresh air and sunshine. Therefore, no moviegoing or even television watching was allowed during daylight except when the weather was bad. Bad meant rain or freezing cold. Since we saw no hope at all for cold that spring, Woodrow and I prayed a lot for rainy Saturdays, because Rocket Man was being serialized, and Tarzan and Roy Rogers took turns as the main feature afterwards. But for reasons unknown to us, God did not want us to see those shows. He did, however, give us an okay on Alfred Hitchcock's *Rear Window* by sending rain one Sunday afternoon.

From Granny's porch after church we gleefully watched the first drops splatter on the walkway.

"Show starts at 1:30," Woodrow said. "We'll just have time to eat dinner first."

In the living room Grandpa and Porter were sharing sections of the Sunday paper, which already had been carefully dissected by Woodrow before church. He had developed a compulsion to be the first one to read the paper on Sunday morning.

Mama and Granny were busy in the kitchen with pot roast and potatoes, biscuits and gravy, peas and carrots.

"Can we help?" Woodrow asked.

Mama and Granny were both startled enough to stop what they were doing and look at him.

"Help in the kitchen?" Granny said. "Boy, have you had a hard lick on the head?"

"The sooner we eat, the sooner we can go to the show," he said.

"The show?" Mama said, and looked out the window. "Oh, I see, it's raining."

She and Granny exchanged one of those amused grown-up looks that said, "Ain't they cute?"

"We'll set the table," Woodrow said.

That's when Porter came in from the living room,

ignorant of our conversation—I think—and said to
Mama, "Let's go see *Rear Window* this afternoon. It
starts at 1:30."

"Oh, is that what's playing?" Mama said as she carried a pitcher of iced tea to the dining-room table
right there beside the kitchen. "I don't care about it,
but the kids are chomping at the bit to go. Why don't
you take them?"

"Yeah!" Woodrow said, without even consulting
me. "Why don'tcha?"

Oh brother. Me and Porter and Woodrow at the
movies together. It was at that precise moment that
my head started to hurt.

"Okay by you, Gyp?" Porter said to me.

Gyp? Now he was going to start in with that buddy-
buddy stuff.

I shrugged and slapped one of Granny's blue willow
plates on the dinner table.

"Reckon so," I mumbled.

What else could I say when it was put to me like
that in a room full of people? I couldn't say I'd rather
stick pins under my fingernails, which I would. There
was a silence you could just about bump into, and I
knew the grown-ups were reviewing the situation; you
know, thinking, When is this young'un going to drop
her grudge against Porter?

Well, I could tell them when—never!

"Isn't it nice of Porter to take y'all to the show?" Granny said too sweetly.

I guess Porter left the room about then, because when I glanced up again he was gone, and Mama with him. I could imagine them discussing the upcoming event and how to manage me.

"How come you don't like Porter?" Woodrow surprised me by asking.

"He makes me sick!" I said, low enough that Granny couldn't hear me.

"I think he's keen," Woodrow said.

Keen? Where'd he pick that one up? Nobody said keen except maybe Jughead in the *Archie* comics.

I slapped six napkins onto the table.

All through dinner Woodrow and Porter jabbered about Alfred Hitchcock, and they didn't ask me what I thought about anything. It was like they were suddenly old pals and I was a bump on a log.

I couldn't eat. I felt nauseous. I had half a mind to stay home. I would. I could practice the piano and do my homework and vacuum Dawg, and help Grandpa listen to the Cleveland Indians on the radio. I wouldn't play with Woodrow when he got home, and I would go to bed early.

But then I would miss Grace Kelly and Jimmy Stewart.

I felt hot. The rain went on. Now I wished it would

stop and the sun would come out, so we couldn't go at all.

Mama was eyeing me. I'll declare she could read my mind.

Porter drove us down to Main Street and parked his car in front of the Ben Franklin Dime Store. Then we walked next door to the theater.

"Three whole tickets, Pearl," Porter said to the little woman in the ticket booth. "I can't get 'em in for half fare anymore. They're both twelve."

"That's what you get for marrying into a ready-made family, Porter Dotson," Pearl said. "That'll be ninety cents."

"Hey, Gypsy," she went on. "Hey, Belle's boy. What's your name again?"

"Woodrow."

"Oh yeah, that's right. I'll remember next time. Did you know I used to sell movie tickets to your mama and your Aunt Love when they weren't even big enough to see up here into the ticket booth?"

"Didja?" Woodrow said. "Did they have to wait for it to rain?"

"Huh?" Pearl said, but Porter was pulling us along, and I was trying to keep up.

I was thinking either I would have to sit between them, in which case Porter would have to be on one side of me, or I would have to put Woodrow between us, in which case Porter would hog all of Woodrow's attention. Putting Porter between me and Woodrow wasn't even an option for me, but it looked like that's what Porter was trying to manipulate when we found three empty seats together in the balcony.

He maneuvered Woodrow into the seat against the wall. Then he started to follow, but I darted in front of him quicker than a hummingbird and got in the middle seat. Porter scratched his head and cleared his throat, but said nothing. I turned my back to him and pulled my knees up to my chin, facing Woodrow.

But it simply was not my day. The two of them leaned in and started talking over my head like I wasn't even present. Then the movie started and nobody talked.

My headache was worse, and I knew I was feverish. I tried my best to concentrate on what was happening in the movie, but the Technicolors started melting together and running down the screen. Jimmy Stewart wavered; Grace Kelly got real, real big, then teeny tiny. She was climbing up the fire escape, fixing to look in the murderer's window, when I remember feeling a sudden panic. My mind went into a fog; I lost my grip and began screaming, "Don't look in there! Don't look in the window!"

Porter was so startled he couldn't move. It was Woodrow who put his hand on my arm and discovered I was burning up with fever.

"She's dying," Woodrow said to Porter, because as

he told me later, he didn't see how anybody could get
so hot and not die.

I went on screaming at Grace Kelly, "Don't look in
there!"

But she didn't hear me. The people trying to watch
the show, however, heard me loud and clear. And
they hollered for me to put a cork in it.

Porter came to his senses, grabbed me up in his
arms, and carried me out, with Woodrow trotting
along behind.

"Call Doc Dot!" Porter yelled at Pearl as we passed
the ticket booth. "Tell him to meet me at my house
straightaway."

I remember sinking . . . sinking . . . I was hot, and
so sad. Don't look in the window. Something ugly is
inside.

It was dark when I opened my eyes to the real world
again. I was in my own bed, and Mama was there
beside me, mopping my face with a cool, wet cloth.
My lamp was on, but a scarf was thrown over the
shade to dim the light.

I didn't remember much of the day.

"Hey," I mumbled, "whatsa matter?"

"Measles," Mama said. "A very bad case."

Was that all? Every pore of my body ached right
down to my hair follicles. Even my eyelids were sore.
And she called it the measles.

"Where's Woodrow?" I said.

"Grandpa took him back to the 7:30 show."

"Why? Did we miss something?"

Mama smiled. "You could say that. Woodrow can tell you how it ended."

Right then I didn't really care. I had never felt so bad.

"Porter is in bed, too," Mama said. "Doc had to give him a sedative."

"How come?"

"You scared him nearly to death. You were delirious, you know, and he thought you were having some kind of fit."

"Do I have to go to school tomorrow?"

"Oh no, you won't be going back until September. When this term is over next week, you will have to stay in bed, and in the dark, for at least ten more days."

"In the dark?"

"Well, only dim light. No reading. Measles has been known to settle in the eyes."

All that night I had strange dreams and hallucinations. One time I thought I had these little-bitty green slits for eyes like a lizard's. And then I dreamed of Blind Benny wandering around town singing.

"It's not so bad being blind," he told me. "I don't have to look at ugly things."

And the old nightmare came and went like a bat

swooping down on me, then retreating into the dark musty caves of my memory. Each time I woke up in a frenzy, my mama was there, calm and cool and beautiful. She sat by me all night long, and the next day she stayed home with me. She made arrangements to take off that whole week from her teaching job to take care of me. Porter, Granny, and Grandpa came in one at a time, but I didn't feel like visiting with them. Doc Dot came around 10:00 and took my temperature. He and Mama went out into the hallway and talked about me.

". . . nightmares." I heard part of what Mama said. "Don't look in the window."

". . . her father" was part of Doc's response.

I put my pillow over my head.

Mama brought my meals and put azaleas and honeysuckle sprigs on my tray. I thought that was real sweet of her, and I was sad that I didn't feel like eating or talking to her.

Late that evening I opened my eyes and there was Woodrow just about a foot above me, his crossed eyes looking into my face.

"When you said Porter makes you sick, you weren't foolin', were you?" he said.

I tried to smile.

"How you feel?" came the inevitable question.

"Well, one minute I'm afraid I'm going to die, and the next minute I'm afraid I'm not."

He grinned. We had heard that line from Minnie Pearl on *The Grand Ole Opry* last Saturday night.

Woodrow sat down in a chair beside my bed.

"You've heard the expression 'cute as a speckled pup'?" he said.

"Sure."

"Well, that's what comes to mind when I look at you, Gypsy."

He was trying to be nice.

"Am I speckled?" I said.

"You're one big speckle, nearabout," he said. "Wanna mirror?"

"No."

"Wanna know how the show ended?"

"To tell you the truth, Woodrow, I don't remember how it started."

"Oh."

"Okay, time for medicine," Mama said as she came in with a small glass of something liquid.

"What's that?" Woodrow said.

"Just a little hot rum to help Gypsy sleep. Doc Dot ordered it."

"Wow! Rum!" Woodrow said. "Wonder why Daddy didn't give me some of his rum when I had the measles."

He watched, fascinated, as Mama helped me sit up and drink the rum.

"How is it?" he said to me.

"Awful!" I said, because it was.

"Daddy always mixed it with apple cider or pop. He said that made it taste better."

Mama gave me a quick drink of water.

"We'll remember that next time," she said to Woodrow. "There now. Time for rest. Visiting hours are over."

"Oh sure," Woodrow said, and stood up. " 'Nite, Gypsy."

" 'Nite, Woodrow."

And that was the end of the worst part of having the measles.

Eleven

It was the next evening just after it got dark that Woodrow came to my window and called softly, "Gypsy, you awake?"

The window was right beside the bed and the curtains were pushed back to let in the night breeze.

"Yeah, I'm awake," I said, rising up on my knees.

Together Woodrow and I removed the screen and eased it down to the floor.

"Are you better?" he said.

"Some," I said. "Doc says my fever's down."

"Had your rum tonight?" he said, grinning.

"Not yet. Mama'll bring it in a while."

"Well, I got somebody here wants to visit you."

"Oh? Who?"

I leaned toward the window and detected a figure about a head taller than Woodrow standing in the shadows.

"I hope he's had the measles," I said.

"Oh yeah. He's had everything," Woodrow said as he pushed the person forward. "Say hello to Blind Benny."

I was flabbergasted.

For years I had heard him singing, but I had seen him only in the dark from afar while he rummaged through people's leftovers and the dogs sniffed around him. Now here he was. Leave it to Woodrow to bring him right up to my window and introduce him like he was somebody's cousin from Grassy Lick maybe.

Blind Benny moved halfway into the dim light coming from the lamp. I could see his face and the legendary sightless eyes that were almost not there. They were like two little holes in his face, about the size of dimes, and not eyes at all. It was an automatic reflex for me to shrink from anything so hideous. I almost gasped, but I clapped a hand over my mouth before the hateful sound could escape.

As usual nothing got past Woodrow. He saw my reaction and smiled.

"Evenin', Miss Beauty," Blind Benny said shyly. "Hope you're a-feelin' fitter than you wuz."

Beauty? Why did he call me that? A feeling akin to pain came with that name.

"I reckon so," I said, trying to find some words.

"I wuz sorry when your cousin here told me you wuz ailin'. But he said you'd not be skeerd of me like most girls is."

Woodrow and I exchanged a glance.

Suddenly Benny started scratching his thighs and behind.

"Chiggers is awful this year," he said. "I might near wore my fangers down to a nub, jist a-scratchin' myself. Woodrow tells me he knows 'bout chiggers. Knows their ways and their secret places, he sez. He's gonna show me how to keep away from 'em. Do the chiggers git on you much, Miss Beauty?"

"Sometimes," I mumbled.

It was true that there was a bumper crop of chiggers that year. They were tiny, almost microscopic bugs that liked to crawl up under your clothes and burrow into the white, fleshy places where the sun never touches. Big ugly red bumps would pop up where they dug in. And Woodrow did have a peculiar knack for sniffing them out.

Lots of times he'd say to me, "Don't sit there. Chigger convention."

Or, "Don't lean on that tree. Chigger city."

"Yeah, Woodrow's right handy to have around sometimes," I said to Blind Benny.

Woodrow looked at me sideways, like he was wondering if I meant something by that.

"When Woodrow ast me to come over here to your winder," Blind Benny said, "it brung to my mind a mem'ry of your pappy in this very room sanging to you when you's jist a little thang."

"You mean . . . my daddy?" I said.

"Oh yeah," Blind Benny said, moving closer and clutching the window ledge.

I felt a tremor go through me as I shrank away from him.

"Amos Leemaster and me wuz boys together back there in Cold Valley, Kentucky, Miss Beauty."

"Why do you call me that?" I said.

"Beauty? Don't you 'member? It wuz *his* name for you! He always called you Beauty—short for Arbutus. He named you hissef—Gypsy Arbutus Leemaster. He sed he couldn't thank of ary other name to beat it, and he were right!"

I felt sick and I wanted him to go away then, but I didn't know how to say it.

"Benny's going to sing to you, Gypsy," Woodrow said.

I lay back on my pillow and closed my eyes. I knew what the song was going to be before he began.

When the moon comes over the mountain
Every beam brings a dream, dear, of you.

Blind Benny's voice was even more wonderful—
haunting, it was—up close. And I could almost hear
my daddy echoing each line.

> *Once again we stroll 'neath that mountain*
> *Through the rose-covered valley we knew.*
> *Each day is gray and dreary,*
> *But the night is bright and cheery.*
> *When the moon comes over the mountain,*
> *I'm alone with my memories of you.*

"It was Amos's fav'rit song," Benny said softly when
he was finished. "He was a good sanger. Too bad what
happened to him!"

"I'm feeling sick," I interrupted, not quite trusting
my voice. "I want to rest now."

"Why, shore. You sleep, Miss Beauty. And I hope
you'll be well agin soon."

I didn't answer.

I heard Woodrow fumbling around with the screen;
then there was silence.

The next day it turned real hot. Porter came into
my room, ran an extension cord in from the hallway,
and placed an electric fan on my dresser. It was one
of those small wire ones that swivel back and forth. It
felt good. Then he brought in a radio.

"Something to keep you cool and something to occupy your mind," he said.

Mama had cleaned out my stash of books.

"How do you feel?" he went on.

"Like a mushroom," I said irritably. "In a cool, dark place."

Porter tuned the radio to Coal Station.

"Can I get anything else for you?" he said.

I shook my head. Didn't he know that if I wanted anything I wouldn't ask him? He hung around for another minute, then left me alone.

The radio was playing "Hernando's Hideaway." It reminded me of my tree house. I thought I would feel better if I could go there and sit on the tree-house porch and hang my feet above the water and listen to the creek rippling over the rocks.

I remembered the day Daddy built the tree house for me. I was barely big enough to get up the steps, and Mama fussed at Daddy because she said I was too small to climb up there and play. So he promised he would always go with me until I was old enough to go by myself. And he did.

Until he died.

I didn't go back to the tree house until I was ten years old—the day Mama and Porter got married and drove away to Myrtle Beach for their honeymoon. Then I climbed up there and went into the room. It was damp and still smelled like raw lumber. There was a button on the floor, and I picked it up and looked at it for a long time. It was green with little swirls of white running through it like marble. I knew it came off Daddy's green shirt—the one he wore to the volunteer firemen's meetings every Tuesday night.

But I didn't want to think about that anymore.

"Mama!" I yelled, feeling clammy and all out of sorts. "I wanna get up!"

She popped in the door just like she had been standing right out there in the hall. She was wearing a blue sundress with daisies all over it, and her hair was brushed back in its everyday style, with a blue ribbon in it, which made her look like a young girl.

"Don't be silly," she said.

"I wanna go to the tree house."

"You'll do no such thing!"

"Why did you marry Porter?"

It was a nasty thing to say, and popped out of nowhere.

"He's not my daddy!" I said in a low, evil voice. "And he never will be! I hate him!"

I saw a slow flush go over her face, and her lip began to tremble.

"You don't give him a chance," she said in a whisper.

I turned my back to her and covered my head with the sheet.

Mama left the room.

By Saturday I felt lots better, and Woodrow spent most of the day with me. We played checkers, and he read to me from a book called *Lorna Doone*. It was real good. Then he showed me how you could talk into the fan; it was queer the way the rotating blades chopped up the sound waves and made your voice quiver.

"That's how it is when Mama calls my name in my dreams," he said sadly.

"Why do you reckon it sounds like that?" I said.

"It's being filtered through two worlds. Some kind of real strong force field separating the two dimensions."

"Oh, I see," I said, but I didn't see at all, and what's more, I didn't think he did either.

"I think maybe she'll try to contact me another way," Woodrow said.

"Like on the telephone?" I said.

"You're making fun of me!" Woodrow said. "I never thought you'd do that, Gypsy."

"Honest, I didn't mean to," I said, because I didn't, but even so, I was still ashamed of myself.

We didn't have anything to say to each other for a long time, and Woodrow looked so pitiful I couldn't stand it. I thought and thought about what I could say to him to make him feel better. Finally I had it.

"Tell you what, Woodrow, when Mama lets me go outside again, we'll have a wienie roast, okay?"

It worked.

"Oh yeah?" he said, brightening.

"Down by the creek," I went on. "There's a place where Grandpa lets me build a fire sometimes. We'll have it there, and we'll invite Mary Lee and Rita and Buzz, Garnet, Franklin Delano, John Ed, and . . ."

"And Peggy Sue and Willy!" he said excitedly.

After that I got better every day.

Twelve

"I want to sit on the stump!" Buzz insisted when we were all gathered around the fire that Saturday night about the end of June.

It was a perfect evening. Except for a wasper, which Buzz killed, and a few gnats, the insects didn't get on us much. There was only one stump, and for that reason I had suggested we all sit on the ground Indian-fashion. But Buzz could be hardheaded as they come, and he was bound and determined to get his own way. I guess we were all a little chickenhearted when it came to Buzz, because he had a reputation for beating people up.

"Why, certainly!" Woodrow said, as agreeable as all get-out. "If Buzz wants to sit on the stump, let him!"

So whether I liked it or not, Buzz climbed up on the stump. I was disgruntled because it put him way yonder higher than the rest of us and we had to look up to see him. On top of that, he decided he wanted to tell a story. Seemed like everybody had a story these days.

We listened politely as he told us this tale we had all heard before, only he said it happened to his aunt and we knew dern good and well that was a lie. He said one day she went to eat from a can of store-bought tomatoes, and there amongst the tomatoes was a human finger. She got so sick she puked all night long. Then she wrote to the factory where they canned those tomatoes, and sure enough, they said yes, one of their workers there lost a finger when he was on the job, and nobody ever found that finger, but thanks to Buzz's aunt, now they knew what had happened to it, and they sent her a whole case of canned tomatoes—which she didn't want—as a reward.

We told Buzz that was a real good story.

Dawg wiggled in between me and John Ed and gobbled up a wienie somebody had dropped on the ground. Then she sighed and lay down beside me and put her head in my lap.

"Now you tell us a story, Woodrow," Rita said.

"Whatsa matter, Fatty?" Buzz said irritably. "You didn't like my story?"

Rita didn't say anything. She just dropped her head.

"Speaking of fingers being chopped off," Woodrow said quickly, and I noticed he laid a hand gently on Rita's plump, tanned arm, "it reminds me of a good one. It was wintertime two years ago, and cold enough to freeze the Abdominal Snowman . . ."

"It ain't abdominal, it's abominable!" Buzz chided.

"Right," Woodrow went on. "It was a joke, Buzz. Anyway, my Aunt Millie was awful sick. In fact, she was on her deathbed. Me and Daddy and Mama were over there trying to do what we could to help Uncle Russell out, but it happened I was the only one in the room with Aunt Millie at one particular moment when she turned her face to me and said, 'Woody, my boy, dying ain't nothin' but changing your form, like water turns to steam, you know?'

"Then she closed her eyes and died right in front of me. I like to cried my eyes out 'cause I loved her."

Willy Stacy belched real big. He had put away four hot dogs. We were all working on a sucker, which had caused Woodrow to pause and get in a couple of licks.

"So we buried her next day," Woodrow went on. "Uncle Russell didn't have the money for an undertaker and a casket and all, so he made his own coffin out of pine. Aunt Millie always loved the smell of pine. And he lined it with that warm, soft stuff Aunt Millie used to line quilts, to keep her warm, he said. Then he dressed her up in her white wedding dress 'cause it was the only fine thing she had to wear. And he left her diamond ring on her finger because he couldn't get it off. It was just a li'l ol' diamond anyway, but she was always so proud of it. She never took it off from the day she married Uncle Russell, and she would tell folks how he had saved up money for three years and ordered it special from Baltimore.

"We all gathered at the graveyard—the Praters and the Honakers. Aunt Millie was a Honaker before she married Uncle Russell, but don't hold that against her. And all the neighbors came, including the Sloans. I'll tell you how those Sloans are—they wouldn't miss a funeral for anything, especially Bertie and Gertie.

"So we had a graveside service there above the old home place where all the Praters are buried. First, the preacher prayed with us over the open casket. Then we placed holly with the red berries on top of her 'cause there wasn't a flower to be found anywhere in that cold. Next Uncle Russell fastened the lid down with leather ties he had made, lowered her into the hole, and shoveled it full of dirt his own self while we all cried; then it started to snow."

There was silence for a moment, except for the frogs and Franklin Delano wheezing. He had the asthma. A little breeze rippled through the apple trees, and an owl hooted. We shivered and moved closer to the fire, just like we could feel that cold winter day Woodrow was talking about.

"Mama and Daddy and me, we went over to Uncle Russell's to fix supper for him and keep him company, for he was tore up pretty good. And when it got dark he said to us, 'Reckon y'all could spend the night?'

"We said we reckoned we could. By ten o'clock it was snowing hard. We stoked the heatin' stove, rolled ourselves up in quilts, and talked quiet-like for a long time, mostly about Aunt Millie."

Woodrow's voice grew soft.

"There was a nice smell in the room that somehow seemed to belong to her, and there were shadows on the walls, and I wondered, Was she close by? Could she hear us? Hadn't she said death is no more than changing forms? So maybe she was one of them shadows or a whiff of whatever that was smelling so good.

"Then Uncle Russell took the one bed, Mama and Daddy took the other, and that left me to sleep on the floor in front of the heatin' stove. But I didn't mind. I thought I could keep the fire burning all night.

"I'll never forget it. My old dog, Moses, had recently died, and I still missed him, so I was dreaming about him when it seemed like I heard somebody calling my name—'Woody'—kinda soft. Then the voice said, 'Woody, I'm so cold.' And again, 'Woody.'

"Well, there was only one person in the world who called me Woody, and you know who that was?"

"Who?" we all said at the same time, but we knew who.

"Aunt Millie! Nobody else ever called me Woody except for her. I woke up shivering and pulled the quilt tighter around me and listened, but all was quiet. Out the window near me I could see snow coming down thick. Then I knew something wadn't right. I could feel a cold draft, and I thought the door musta blowed open, so I rolled over and looked at the front door. Then I like to died. She was standing there in the open doorway."

"Who!"

"Aunt Millie!"

"Her ghost?"

"That's what I thought—a ghost! But it was really her standing there in that white dress with snow all over her hair and blood all over her front."

"Blood?"

"Yeah, blood. She was looking right at me and holding out one hand toward me. It was that hand that was bleeding.

" 'Woody,' she said. 'I'm so cold.'

"And I started hollerin.' How would you feel if you saw a dead woman standing in the doorway at night in the snow calling your name? Well, I'll tell you one thing right now, you wouldn't feel good about it. And if I'd been an old person like Granny or Grandpa, I woulda had a heart attack on the spot. I about did anyhow.

"Mama and Daddy and Uncle Russell came rushing in, and when they saw Aunt Millie, all three of them froze where they stood. I'll declare, the natural laws of the world seemed reversed. You couldn't believe your eyeballs.

"It was Uncle Russell who came to his senses first. He grabbed her and brought her in to the heatin' stove.

" 'My darlin's come back to me,' he said.

"When it was all sorted out, what happened was this: The Sloan sisters, Bertie and Gertie, saw that diamond ring on Aunt Millie's finger at the graveside service and decided to dig her up, take the ring, fill the grave again, and nobody would know the difference. But when they tried to get the ring, it wouldn't come off her finger. So they took a knife and cut her finger off.

"That's when Aunt Millie rose up and shouted, 'What the hell you doin' to me?'

"And that scared Bertie and Gertie so bad they ran away screaming, and Aunt Millie crawled out of the grave. She was a little bit out of her head and didn't rightly know what was happening, but she knew how to get home."

"How could that happen?" Garnet said. "Did she come back to life?"

"Shoot no, Garnet, she never was dead to start with. We buried her alive. But she sure seemed dead. Bertie and Gertie Sloan actually saved her life by trying to rob her grave."

"Well, did she die then?" Franklin Delano wanted to know.

"Nope. That night Uncle Russell took her to the Clinch Valley Clinic, where they stitched up her hand and kept her for a while. Then they sent her home. She's alive and kicking to this very day."

"And what about Bertie and Gertie?" John Ed said.

"Both of them, their hair turned white overnight. And the next time anybody saw them, they were down at the Church of Jesus getting saved. They swore never to steal anything again, and they sent Aunt Millie's ring back to her by way of the preacher. They had put it in a li'l ol' aspirin tin with cotton all around it. 'Course Aunt Millie had to wear it on her pinkie after that. But she said that was a small price to pay for her life."

"Is that the truth, Woodrow, or did you make it up?" Buzz said.

"It's the truth, Buzz. It really happened. You're always wanting to know is something really the truth," Woodrow said.

"Well, I like to know," Buzz said. "I don't like stories that somebody made up."

We didn't say a word about his canned-tomatoes story.

"Now I have another story," Buzz announced. "It's about a rabid squirrel. It's a true story, too."

"Hold on there," Peggy Sue said. "Which one was it, a rabbit or a squirrel?"

With that we got hysterical, and started telling jokes one on top of another. Woodrow wanted me to tell the eyeball one, but everybody had already heard it, so I asked him to tell the two-tents one, which he did, and everybody liked it. In the midst of this carrying on and acting a fool, I glanced up at Buzz and I saw he was not laughing at all. Huh-oh. Somebody musta stepped on his corns real hard. He was looking at Woodrow like he might want to clobber him.

"Hey, Woodrow," he hollered suddenly. "Was your mama cross-eyed?"

Those foul words fell like a wet blanket on our good time. Nobody said anything for the longest time. I guess we were trying to think of something to say that wouldn't make Buzz madder or insult Woodrow either.

"No," Woodrow said at last. "Just me."

"Oh well, where'd you get 'em?" Buzz went on. "Maybe them cockeyed stories the girls seem to like so much crossed your goofy eyes, huh?"

We had interrupted his story about a rabid squirrel.

It was plain we really didn't care about his stories, and he was jealous of Woodrow.

"Well, I'll tell you," Woodrow said brightly. "When they were giving out looks, I thought they said books, and I said, 'Give me a funny one!' "

That got us started again. It was like the knock-knock jokes. Everybody had one.

"When they were giving out brains," Peggy Sue chimed in, "I thought they said pains, and I said, 'Don't give me any.' "

"When they were giving out noses, I thought they said roses, and I said, 'Give me a big red one!' " Willy said.

And around and around it went. I stole a peep at Woodrow. He seemed to be having a good time still.

It was after everybody left that I said to him, "Sorry about Buzz, Woodrow. Next time we'll not even ask him."

"Oh shoot! Don't worry about Buzz," Woodrow said cheerfully. "He won't have time to give us any trouble for a while. He'll be too busy scratching."

"What do you mean?" I said.

"You know that stump he just *had* to sit on?"

"Yeah."

"It was chiggers national headquarters."

Thirteen

The next morning it rained early on; then the sun came out bright, and a warm steam rose up from the ground. I loved to go mushing through the grass when it got like that. But if I wasn't careful I would step on an earthworm. They were crawling up to the sun to tan their slinky pink bodies on the walkway or rocks or any bare place they could find.

"Catch me some fat, juicy ones, Gypsy," Grandpa said, as he took his toolbox around the side of the house. "There's some baby birds out there in the orchard and I'm thinking their mama died. We'll go feed 'em."

"Oooo, no, I'm not about to put my fingers on

them," I said, sounding for all the world like Mama. "Maybe Woodrow will do it when he comes back."

When the rain stopped, Granny and Woodrow had walked to the Piggly Wiggly to buy groceries. I was practicing the piano when they left or I would have gone with them.

I followed Grandpa around to where he was fixing some shaky railing on his wraparound first-floor porch. He was on the Slag Creek side, on his knees nailing a brace against a rail. I got down beside him and commenced handing nails to him.

"Grandpa, how come the way a person looks is so important?" I said.

"A person had orta put up a good appearance, I reckon," he said.

Even though Grandpa was a schoolteacher at one time and knew better, he sometimes let his grammar slide back to the way he talked when he was a boy on the top of Wiley Mountain. He called it his everyday voice.

"But what if there's something a person can't help?" I said, raising my voice to the normal shout.

"Like what?" he shouted back.

"Like crooked teeth," I said. "You can't help them."

"You could get braces," Grandpa came back.

"Well, supposing I had a big wart on my nose?" I said.

"Doc would take it off for nothing," Grandpa said.

"He's good about stuff like that, and the Lord knows, we wouldn't have our pretty Gypsy going around town with a wart on her nose."

"What about crossed eyes?" I said.

"Oh," Grandpa said. "Is somebody poking fun at Woodrow?"

"Yeah," I said. "Buzz Osborne. He's so mean."

"You never could tell them Osbornes a dadblamed thing. No need to try," Grandpa said.

"It seems like anytime a person wants to hurt another person's feelings, he says nasty things about his looks," I said, exasperated. "What possible difference could it make how a person looks if he is a good person?"

"It shouldn't make no difference a'tall," Grandpa said. "But it does to most folks."

"Being good-looking ain't everything," I went on. "Look at Eleanor Roosevelt. She's plain, but she's the most wonderful person. And she's accomplished so much. Miss Hart says it makes her proud to be a woman."

"And Miss Hart's right as rain," Grandpa said. "And look also at Abraham Lincoln. I reckon an uglier man was never born. But see what-all he did for his country."

Then Grandpa smiled and patted me on the head.

"But a pretty girl like you sure is nice to look at, Gypsy."

"Mama cares more about my looks than I do," I said. "She's the one wants me to have this mane."

"Well, I'll tell you right now, girl, that mane, as you call it, is a sight. Everybody has something to say about your hair."

"Let's say I took a notion to cut it. Ain't it my hair? Can't I cut it if I want to?"

"Why would you want to go and do a thing like that for?"

"Because it's so much trouble. I hate taking care of it."

"I gotta feeling that would be a thing up with which your mama would not put," Grandpa said.

That was one of Grandpa's little jokes—mocking what he thought were silly rules of grammar, like not ending a sentence with a preposition.

"The most important question still is: What does it matter how pretty or ugly a person is?" I said seriously.

"You got me," he said.

Then Grandpa laid down his hammer and pulled one of those big red bandana handkerchiefs out of his back pocket. He sat down flat on the porch beside me, removed his glasses, and started to clean them. This was a signal to me that Grandpa was fixing to say something important.

"I'll tell you a thing, Gypsy, that your mama probably never did tell you," he said softly.

"Shoot," I said.

"It was your daddy's idea to have your hair grow out so long and silky and shiny."

Grandpa stopped talking and touched my pigtails.

"You were only five when he died, but even then you were a picture. I recall it was one day during his last few weeks that he said to your mama, 'Love, promise me you'll never cut my Beauty's hair.'

"And Love promised. So that's why she won't hear of cutting it."

I didn't speak, because this big thing was stuck in my craw so that I had to swallow and swallow and blink and blink. It was akin to that day Granny told me about my daddy ". . . come riding over Cold Mountain on a black horse . . . big as life . . . so tall and straight in the saddle . . ."

"Now," Grandpa went on matter-of-factly, like we could have been discussing just any old body. "Appearances are just that, Gypsy—appearances, and not the genuine self. When I was teaching school, I noticed the best-looking girls and boys could be mean as copperheads, and the ugliest ones could be as good-hearted as they come. But that's not to say either that a pretty person can't be good, too. They can . . . like your mama. Or that an ugly person can't be bad. They can that, too. But it's only what's in the heart that counts."

"Then why do folks even notice Woodrow's eyes? Anybody can see how good he is. He's so much fun and he knows so many stories. And he treats everybody like they're special."

"I know," Grandpa said. "He is good like you say, and he is sensitive, too, like Belle was. She wanted more than anything to be pretty like your mama, but she just wasn't. And folks were always comparing them. Right in front of Belle they'd talk about what a beauty Love was.

"When she ran away with Everett Prater, she was feeling low . . . like she couldn't do any better—not that there's anything wrong with Everett. Nothing a'tall. But Belle didn't even know him. And she hadn't a clue what she was getting into, moving up in the shadow of those hills where the sun don't even shine till noon.

"And here with us she had everything she needed and lots of things she wanted besides. We had hopes of sending her out into the world to study piano with the best of them. She was better than good. You're a lot like her in that way, Gypsy."

I was surprised and pleased. It was the first time Grandpa had ever mentioned my piano playing. And it reminded me that nobody ever bragged on me for anything except my looks. And they couldn't say enough about that. Yeah, I guess somebody might oc-

casionally comment on the fact that I could tell a
good joke, but how nice it would be to be admired, I
thought, because I am interesting like Woodrow, or
talented or smart . . . anything but just pretty. There
had to be more important things than just being
pretty. Then it occurred to me that that was an easy
thing for a pretty girl to say. With poor Aunt Belle
there was nothing more important. So what was the
answer? I was confused.

I became aware that Grandpa's voice was becoming
agitated and louder.

"It was Belle's choice," he was saying, "to go live
the old-timey ways with Everett's clan. We went to
see her, your granny and me, but she never made us
feel welcome. Then she took to hiding from us when
she saw us coming.

" 'Tell them I died,' she'd say to Everett. Just being
sassy, you know. But Everett would repeat to us what
she said. And it hurt your granny's feelings so bad,
she'd cry. It did nothing but irritate the fool out of
me.

"Then Woodrow was born, and we went to see him.
She was nicer to us, so we went back now and again.
And we would give her books, because that was the
only thing she would take from us.

"We figured out she was embarrassed with her living
conditions, so we didn't go as often. Ever' now and

then we'd bump into her and Woodrow down on Main Street doing some shopping, and she was friendly enough. Then one Decoration Day the two of them came to the ceremonies at the cemetery to put flowers on the family graves.

"After your daddy died, she started coming to visit once in a while, and your mama took you up there to play with Woodrow occasionally. I thought maybe Belle and Love would make up and be friends, like sisters should be, but it never happened.

"She never confided in Love or any of us how she was feeling. If she needed anything, if she was sorry or blue or wanting to come home. When you'd ask her how things were, she'd answer fine, things were fine. Everett was fine. The baby was fine."

Grandpa cleared his throat and ran his hand over his balding head.

"If she had said something. Any little hint. We would have done anything for her. We thought the world and all of her."

"Well, Grandpa, maybe she was happier than you thought she was," I said, although I knew from what Woodrow had said that that wasn't true.

"No, child, no. I never believed for a minute she was happy with him. That union was doomed, because it was an impulsive, foolish thing, and I'm betting they both regretted it."

"But she would never say she regretted it, Grandpa?"

"No, she was too proud. But she never said she was happy either. What she did say was nothing. Just nothing. Not to us. Maybe I'll never know what was on her mind."

"Grandpa, do you think it's possible . . . Well, I almost hate to say it, but . . ."

"Spit it out," Grandpa said.

"Do you reckon Uncle Everett might've had something to do with Aunt Belle's disappearance?"

Grandpa looked at the sky and said nothing. I guess he was trying to decide what he really did believe. I was thinking of the blond-headed woman I had seen in Uncle Everett's Ford, but I didn't know if Grandpa had seen her or not.

"Well?" I hurried him. "Do you?"

Then there came a big fat *"No!"* not from Grandpa, but from Woodrow, who was near us in the yard. He had come home and walked around the house. There was no telling how long he had been listening. And it was a sure thing he had heard everything we said, because you couldn't help hearing around this place where the volume was always wide open.

"No!" Woodrow said again. "Don't you dare say that!"

" 'Course not, Woodrow," Grandpa said gently. "We don't believe such a thing."

Woodrow turned on his heel like a top and stalked across the yard toward Slag Creek.

Me and Grandpa just looked at each other, stunned and ashamed.

"I guess we orta apologize," Grandpa said.

I agreed.

Fourteen

I left Woodrow alone for a while, went home to undo my pigtails and wash my hair, then searched him out. He was inside the tree house, cutting out personal ads from some old Sunday newspapers he had saved and placing the ads carefully inside my jewelry box, where we had commenced keeping our treasures.

"You sore at me, Woodrow?"

"Naw. I ain't sore."

I parked on the floor beside him.

"We need some furniture in here," I said. "Something to sit on."

"Yeah," he said. "Granny is going to give us her old blue rug soon as she gets a new one."

"Wanna go feed some baby birds whose mama died?" I said.

"Sure. Feed 'em what?"

"Worms. You have to pick them up. I don't want to."

Woodrow almost smiled.

"Why are you saving those ads, Woodrow?"

"I dunno. I just think they're interesting. You know, folks send messages to each other sometimes through these ads?"

"Do they? Like what? Let me see."

Woodrow spread out one of the papers, and we fell down side by side to read it.

"Here's one," Woodrow said. "Lizzie baby, call Charlie 9147."

"What if Lizzie baby never reads the paper?" I said.

"Then Charlie wasted his quarter," Woodrow said. "Listen here to this one: Clyde Higgins is no longer responsible for the debts of Myrtle Higgins."

"Free dog," I read aloud. "Don't bark after 10:00 p.m."

"Smart dog," Woodrow said. "He can tell time."

"Looking for family roots," I read. "All Stiltners call me at Cedar 3291, Rising Sun, Maryland."

"That guy has no idea how many Stiltners live here," Woodrow said. "His phone will never stop ringing. They run these ads only on Sunday. Aunt Millie let us have her paper when she was done with it, and

Mama and I would read these ads together. We got a lotta laughs out of 'em. We would read the *Katzenjammer Kids* and *Li'l Abner*. Then we'd do the crossword puzzle, but the ads were our favorite."

"I'm sorry, Woodrow," I said; then added quickly, "Grandpa is, too."

"What? Oh well, that's okay."

"Woodrow, do you know where the poem says, *People are going back and forth across the doorsill / where the two worlds touch?*"

"Yeah?"

"Do you think the two worlds could mean her life here with Grandpa and Granny, and her life there with you and Uncle Everett?"

"Mama was always fascinated with that place where two different things come together."

"What do you mean?"

"Like twilight and dawn—places where dark and light meet. Like the horizon. Like the moment between waking and sleeping. See what I mean?"

"I think so."

"She talked to me a lot about those few seconds just before I was born when she went out of her body and met me.

" 'We were hovering between this side and the other side,' she'd say to me. 'And it was right on the stroke of midnight, too, between the old year and the new.' She thought that was real significant.

"And once she said how odd it would be to live on the equator, or exactly on the place where a time zone changes. She was peculiar that way."

"Yeah, but in the poem . . ."

"In the poem," Woodrow interrupted me, "it's talking about that place I told you about where two worlds touch."

"So you really think she's in that other place . . . in another world?" I said.

"I know she is. A whole 'nother world."

He folded the newspaper neatly and tossed it on the splintery floor.

Then how come he was so interested in checking the ads every Sunday, I was thinking, but I didn't say it. Because it all fit together—Woodrow's great interest in the newspaper every Sunday and no other day. He was looking for his mother to send him a message through the classified ads. So he really didn't believe his own farfetched story. He felt she was somewhere in this world, and she would contact him in a familiar way.

Fifteen

In midsummer the apples were getting some size to them. They were bending the tree branches down, and you could smell them when the breeze was just right. But you couldn't eat them yet, because they were too bitter. Woodrow tried it and got a fearful bellyache.

There were blackberries and raspberries growing wild along the creek bank. And from Grandpa's patch of garden in that sunny place behind the shed, butter beans and green beans, summer squash, tender cucumbers, and melons of all shapes and sizes were coming on.

It was the best time of year for good stuff to eat. There were always fresh berry pies cooling on the kitchen windowsills, and there was corn bread to crumble up in your vegetables, and fried green tomatoes and okra. You could drink cold buttermilk with your roastin' ears, and dribble hot pork drippings over your garden salad. There was nothing like it.

It was also the time of year for Mama's annual garden party, the social event of the season. It was always written up as such in the *Mountain Echo*'s social section. In the past I had dreaded it worse than a typhoid shot, but that summer of 1954 was different, because Woodrow was there. He was interested in everything and almost everybody, and the way he looked at things with fresh eyes made me see them fresh, too.

It was an especially hot, humid summer afternoon the second week of July. Grandpa and Porter moved tables and chairs down by Slag Creek at the edge of the orchard near the tree house. The gardenias there were in full bloom and aroma. It was my favorite flower. Sometimes I could smell it in my dreams.

It was mine and Woodrow's job to get all the names of the women there and make sure they were spelled right for the newspaper. We were also in charge of serving refreshments, which consisted of dainty sandwiches of exotic substances, mints, nuts, and Mama's special drink, which she named Peach Ice. It was made with vanilla ice cream, fresh peaches, and ginger ale.

Mama had me wear a plain white, sleeveless cotton

dress with a real fancy ruffled red apron, red sandals, and red ribbons in my hair. Everybody oooed and ahhed over me. Woodrow was wearing a short-sleeved white shirt, black pants, and a red bow tie, and he took his job very seriously. He wouldn't let anybody run out of anything.

There were about fifty women there, counting Mama and Granny and the five eighteen-year-old debutantes who were coming out that year. That meant they were now considered young women of marriageable age and could be included in all the right gatherings with the other women who had a certain social standing in town. It was a tradition that went way back, all the way across the water to the old countries. Since Coal Station was a mining town, I asked Mama one time how come none of the miners' daughters were ever invited to be a debutante. Mama just looked at me and said, "When you're a debutante yourself, you'll understand."

I figured I wouldn't be a debutante if I could help it, but to say that to Mama would be like saying I didn't want to live past the age of eighteen.

Woodrow was immediately smitten with the debutantes, so I let him serve them. They really were pretty and smelled almost as good as the gardenias. They were all wearing sweet sundresses in pastel colors, with crinolines underneath, high heels, summer hats, and white gloves, which they very carefully removed before eating the delectables Woodrow spread before them. They fussed over Woodrow and called him "darling" and "dearest" and "precious," which were not your routine Coal Station words. Woodrow soaked them up like sunshine.

Mrs. Osborne, Buzz's mama, was a jolly, wee woman, who favored Mammy Yokum in *Li'l Abner* the way she jerked herself around like a puppet and tended to wrap her arms and legs around her own self, and the way she smoked cigarettes one after the other. Buzz, her oldest boy, was her favorite topic of conversation; whether anybody was listening or not made no difference to her.

"He had such a case of the scratchies a while back," she said at one point. "I don't know if it was poison ivy or chiggers—or maybe even the itch. He never would let me see it."

Woodrow and I looked at each other with perfectly straight faces.

Mrs. Cooper, the principal's wife, who had grabbed Woodrow under the chin that first day at church, said, "It's no tellin' what a child might pick up going to school with those hillbillies."

She complimented me nearly to death, patting me on the head like I was a poodle, and called Woodrow Angel Face till I thought he would puke on her if she said it again. But when Mama was far enough away, and seeing to the needs of her guests, Mrs. Cooper leaned over casually and said to Woodrow, "What do you hear from your mama, boy?"

Woodrow's face flushed.

Mrs. Cooper would never have said a thing like that in front of my mama, Love Ball Dotson, sister to Belle Prater and leader of Coal Station's social set.

"Nothin'," Woodrow mumbled, and tried to move on.

"And I doubt you ever will!" she called after him. "She was an impulsive thing! Hard to tell what she's done this time!"

The debutantes who were standing nearby looked away and pretended they didn't hear or see, but they did. And Woodrow knew they did.

I watched him walk toward Mama's kitchen.

"She called me a cow, you know," Mrs. Cooper said to me.

"Who did?" I said.

I was thinking to myself I would never insult a cow in that manner, but I didn't say such a thing.

"Belle Ball!" Mrs. Cooper went on. "She was in the ninth grade and I was her English teacher. She said it right in front of Mr. Cooper. That was before we were married. I'll never forget it. And I said to myself then and there, 'This girl will never amount to a hill of beans!' And you see? I was right!"

So that was it! As a young girl Aunt Belle had embarrassed her in front of her boyfriend. And Mrs.

Cooper had carried that anger with her all these years, so that now it was a bitter acid she was spraying on Woodrow in retaliation.

Woodrow came back shortly with a trayful of tall, frosted glasses of Peach Ice and resumed his duties as if nothing had happened. I saw him lean over and whisper to one of the pretty debutantes where she sat on a pink blanket. She giggled and I was thinking, Well, what do you know about that. Woodrow is learning to flirt.

Then I got busy—real busy. In fact, I couldn't keep up. Every time I surfaced for air, somebody needed something else. I made about a hundred trips to Granny's kitchen, where Grandpa was doing all he could to help without actually going amongst the "hens," as he called them. It didn't occur to me to be insulted. The women did put you in mind of a whole lot of hens.

I noticed Woodrow was trotting pretty regular to Mama's kitchen, where the ice was stored in the freezer and the Peach Ice filled up the Frigidaire. It was so hot everybody was drinking a lot of it. I saw him offer Mrs. Cooper some and then whisper something to her. Mrs. Cooper clapped one hand over her mouth to stifle a sputter and reached for the glass with the other.

One thing was sure: Woodrow would not be flirting with Mrs. Cooper! So what was going on? As I stood there puzzling over it, Granny whispered to me, "Mrs. Osborne is trying to eat and smoke and talk about Buzz all at the same time, and she is dribbling. Can you fetch her a napkin?" So I got busy again.

As the sun moved across the sky, the women clucked louder and got happier, especially Mrs. Cooper. She slipped into a fine mood. She was laughing and complimenting people, talking about how much she liked first this one, then that one; which was not a bit like Mrs. Cooper to go on like that. Why, she was as pleasant as Mrs. Santa Claus. But the thing that beat all was the way she and Woodrow buddied up. Every time he would bring her a fresh glass of Peach Ice—and she really was putting it away—she would giggle like a girl. She even started reminiscing out loud.

"Me and my sister, Audrey—she's a nurse in Roanoke, you know—used to wade up the creek on a hot day like this and gather tiger lilies. We had the best times."

"That sounds like fun, Mrs. Cooper," Woodrow said.

"I wish I could wade in the creek again," she went on wistfully.

"I wisht you could, too," Woodrow said sweetly, and patted her on the shoulder.

In light of that conversation I shouldn't have been

surprised a little while later to hear Mrs. Cooper's voice down by the creek near the tree house, but I was.

"Come on in! It's wunnerful!"

I eased my way through the powdered and perfumed ladies on the creek bank, and there I saw Mrs. Cooper with her dress tail pulled up to her thighs. This was the same Mrs. Cooper who, in the past, lay awake nights thinking up ways to put a stop to folks' fun.

"Come on in, girls! Don't be proud!"

And she giggled.

The other women stood on the bank, uncertain, not knowing if they should be embarrassed for Mrs. Cooper or laugh, jump in with her, or what. You could almost hear the whirling in their very proper heads. There was nothing in the etiquette books about creek wading at an elegant garden party.

"I'll declare, Gypsy," Granny whispered to me for the second time that day. "If I didn't know better, I'd say she's drunk!"

Drunk! Of course! The bottle of rum in our kitchen! That's why Woodrow kept running in there. He had gone and got Mrs. Cooper drunk!

"Oh no, Granny," I said in the most scandalized voice I could find. "Mrs. Cooper doesn't drink!"

Suddenly one of the debutantes kicked off her white pumps.

"What the heck!" she said, as she gathered up her pretty dress tail and crinoline in a bunch and went splashing into the creek. "I'm hot!"

"Me too!"

It was Mrs. Osborne jumping in.

Did he put rum in all the Peach Ice?

Then another debutante. *"Geronimo!"*

Mrs. Cooper was laughing so hard she suddenly lost her footing and went flying backwards into the water, wetting herself all over. The two debutantes, also laughing and splashing, went to her aid and, in the process, went down, too.

And there they were. Somehow it didn't quite fit the picture of the Event of the Season, as it was usually referred to in the social column of the *Mountain Echo.* I looked around for Mama. She was standing back a piece from the other spectators, her pink polished fingernails resting lightly at her pretty white throat—totally dumbfounded.

Woodrow was standing a few feet away from me, watching the four women in the water and enjoying himself immensely.

I eased over to him. "Woodrow, did you put rum in Mrs. Cooper's Peach Ice?"

"No, Gypsy," he said calmly. "I did not."

"Then what . . . how?"

"Just an experiment I wanted to try with the power of suggestion," he said, and his eyes lit up again.

"What kind of experiment?" I said.

"You see, there was no rum involved—no alcohol at all. What I did, see, I told Mrs. Cooper that her drink had a bit of rum in it. Her mind did the rest. I didn't figure on her going splashing around in the creek like that."

And Woodrow laughed out loud.

"What about the debutantes?" I said. "And Mrs. Osborne? What did you tell them?"

"Oh, them? Nothin'. They're just hot, so they're cooling off."

Sixteen

"Now, let me get this straight, Woodrow," Doc Dot said. "You told Mrs. Cooper her drink was laced with rum, but it really wasn't."

"That's right. I would never slip alcohol into a person's drink. I know it could hurt them," Woodrow said with such sincerity you had to believe him.

Mama, Porter, Granny, Grandpa, Doc Dot, Woodrow, and I were all seated around our kitchen table late that evening. The rum bottle, still three-quarters full, had earlier been produced, viewed, and tasted to verify it was the real stuff, and returned to its respectable place on the medicine shelf. It was agreed Woodrow had not been into the rum, but he was still getting the third degree.

"And you're saying it was an experiment?" Porter said.

"Yeah. Me and Mama read one time that the power of the mind is so strong that if you tell a person he is drinking liquor and he really believes it, he might feel the effects just like if he is drinking alcohol for sure. We tried it on Daddy by pouring out his rum and putting water in the bottle, but it didn't work with him 'cause Daddy was so used to the taste and the smell and the feelin' of rum, he didn't believe it. You gotta believe it, see? So me and Mama reckoned it would work on somebody that wasn't used to drinking, somebody you could fool into believing, so—"

"Hold it! Hold it!" Granny interrupted loudly. "Back up! Speak up! Slow down!"

Woodrow was breathless.

"You actually said to Mrs. Cooper, 'There is rum in your drink'?" Mama said.

"Yeah. That was the seed I planted, see? I said to her . . ."

Here Woodrow leaned over and spoke in my ear the way I had seen him do with Mrs. Cooper.

"I put some rum in this drink just for you, okay?"

"And she believed me. She asked for more and more."

All eyes were on Woodrow, and once again he had astounded everybody.

"It worked real good on Mrs. Cooper," Woodrow said, blushing a little. "I wisht Mama coulda been here to see. She'd be tickled."

Woodrow let out a satisfied little sigh.

About that time Porter started making funny noises in his throat, and he cupped his hand over his mouth. Then Doc had to bend over and pick something up off the floor. Was he trying to hide his face? Was he laughing? When the men couldn't hold it in any longer, they like to fell out of their chairs. At first Woodrow was startled at the sudden explosion of laughter; then he broke into a sheepish grin. Even Mama and Granny couldn't hold their faces straight.

"I wonder if Mrs. Cooper still believes it?" I said. "Does she still think rum was served at Mama's garden party?"

"Oh my goodness," Mama said. "I wonder."

"It doesn't matter," Porter said, as he pulled out a handkerchief and wiped his eyes. "In the *Echo* we'll say, 'A good time was had by all!' and leave it at that."

Nobody forgot Love Dotson's garden party of '54. As for Woodrow, he shrugged and went on with his life.

It was maddening to me how he could stir up a whole town in a single afternoon and not even get scolded for it and I could never get away with anything at all. I reckon it was about that time I came across a streak of jealousy I didn't know was hiding and festering in me.

In August the apples were changing color. Between the sunshine and the rain they were earning their title—Golden Delicious. You could smell them everywhere. It was a wet month, so wet in fact that we got tired of going to the movies and watching television. We even got tired of each other—Woodrow and me. Conditions were ripe for our first quarrel.

It was on an evening when Uncle Everett came to see Woodrow, but he stayed only about fifteen minutes and was gone. I could tell Woodrow was disappointed. We lay down on the floor and started watching television. A little girl was singing "Pretty Is as Pretty Does."

"That ain't the truth," Woodrow said.

"What ain't the truth?" I said.

"Pretty is as pretty does. That's saying that anybody who *does* pretty *is* pretty, and that ain't the truth."

"No," I disagreed. "I think it's saying you can't be pretty unless you do pretty."

"Pretty people can do anything they want to and get away with it just because they are pretty," he said.

"Well, I guess you're one of them pretty people, Woodrow Prater, 'cause you do anything you want to and get away with it."

"What do you mean by that?" he said.

"The rum! You got away with that without even a scolding from anybody!"

"That's because I didn't do anything!" he said crossly. "If I had really given rum to Mrs. Cooper, that would be different, but I didn't."

"You lied," I said bluntly.

"Lied? How did I lie?"

"You told her she was drinking rum, and that was a lie!"

"Well, excuse me, but how can you carry out an experiment on the power of suggestion without making a suggestion? Huh? Tell me that!"

I had no answer.

The evening news came on, and John Cameron Swayze was showing some scenes of New York City while he did a story. One of the places was a hospital.

"I wonder if that's the one," Woodrow said.

"What are you talking about?" I said.

"There's a famous hospital in New York," Woodrow said, "that operates on people's crossed eyes and makes them straight."

" 'Zat so?"

"Yeah. Mama read me all about it in the newspaper. Me and her were saving money to take me up there and get that operation."

"How much does it cost?"

"Oh, lots. Couple hundred dollars, maybe."

"How much did you save?"

"Not much. Thirty bucks."

"What happened to it?" I said.

"What do you mean, what happened to it?" he suddenly yelled at me, as he raised himself up on his elbows.

I was startled.

"I mean . . . what . . . what happened to the thirty dollars you saved? That's all I meant. Did you have to spend it on something else?"

"That's none of your business!" he sputtered.

There was more anger in his eyes than I had ever seen there before.

"You don't have to know everything!" he went on.

"Well, shut my mouth!" I said.

And I did.

We didn't speak then, and the air seemed to grow thick with our silence.

Coke Time with Eddie Fisher came on, and Eddie started singing "Oh, My Pa-Pa."

"I don't like that song," I said, just trying to make conversation.

"How come?" Woodrow snapped. " 'Cause it reminds you of your daddy?"

"No," I said, surprised that he would mention my daddy. He never had before. "Because it's Porter's favorite song."

"Why are you so mad at Porter?" Woodrow came back. "It wasn't him that left you!"

"My daddy didn't leave me!" I screamed at him. "He died! A person can't help dying, you know!"

"He . . ." Woodrow started to say more, but thought better of it. "Never mind," he mumbled.

I breathed a sigh of relief.

After the rain stopped, we went out on the porch and sat in the swing.

The air smelled clean and sweet. A few stars came out to wink.

Rita and Garnet dropped by, and the four of us sat there in the misty mountain shadows and talked of important things—school starting in a few weeks, new classes and teachers, who liked who, stuff like that.

Dawg came and nestled her head against me. I scratched behind her ears.

"Do you have a story for us, Woodrow?" Rita asked sweetly.

Woodrow sighed.

"Yeah, I got one."

Didn't he always?

"Way back in the hollers a long time ago," he began, "there was a beautiful girl with long, golden hair."

"Like Gypsy," Garnet said.

"She was married to a farmer," Woodrow continued, ignoring Garnet's comment, "and he wasn't good enough for her. In fact, she thought nobody was good enough for her—at least not in these hills. Then one day a city slicker named Leon came along and asked the girl to go away with him. Her name was Olive Ann, by the way. So Olive Ann said yes, she would go away with him, but first he would have to kill the farmer, because he would come find her and drag her right back. So they plotted to kill the farmer in his sleep.

"But you see, what they didn't know was, the farmer overheard them plotting. And you can figger he was plenty sore. So when they came to kill him that night, he was ready for them, and he killed them instead with his hunting rifle.

"The farmer took Leon's body and dumped it down an old abandoned mining shaft, but he couldn't bear to do that with Olive Ann's body, because she was so beautiful and he still loved her, even though she treated him like a dog. So he buried her in his own back yard under the grass.

"When folks missed Olive Ann and asked the farmer where she had got to, the farmer told them she had gone down to Cincinnati to see some kinfolks, and that satisfied them for a while. But as time went by and she didn't come back, they got suspicious, especially since the city slicker had disappeared, too. Not only that, but the farmer's conscience started hurting him bad. He cried a lot, and talked about Olive Ann to anybody who would listen.

"Then one day the farmer looked out the window and saw something that nearabout scared him senseless. Out there where he buried Olive Ann, there was golden hair growing out of the ground where the grass used to be!

"The farmer went out there and cut that hair right down close to the ground before somebody might see it, but next morning it had growed longer than before and covered more ground.

"You can bet he was frantic. So he cut the hair again, but before the day was over, it had growed back even longer and covered more ground still.

"A week later the sheriff came out there to ask the farmer about Olive Ann, and what he found made him shiver.

"The whole hillside there was covered with long, golden hair just a-blowin' in the wind. And in the middle of it was the farmer. The hair was all growed up around him in a tangled knot, and it had squeezed the life out of him."

There was silence when Woodrow finished his story.

"Well, didn't you like it?" he said crossly.

"It sure was strange," Rita said.

"Is it true?" said Garnet.

" 'Course not!" Woodrow said irritably. "It's a story with a moral."

"And what is the moral?" Rita said.

"The moral is, don't ever have anything to do with a girl with long, golden hair. She'll tie you up in knots every time."

With those words I got up, stomped across the porch, and went home.

"Damn dern it!" I sputtered as I stepped up on my own porch. "Double damn dern it!"

"Damn dern it?" came an echo from the shadows of the porch.

It was Porter sitting there in a chair, smoking a cigarette. "Gypsy, if I couldn't cuss any better'n that, I'd quit trying."

I glared at him.

"Whatsa matter?" he said.

"Why wasn't Woodrow punished for what he did at the garden party?" I said angrily.

"Do you think he should have been punished?"

"He thinks he's so clever!" I said. "With his stories and experiments and stuff!"

Porter said nothing.

"If I had done what he did, Mama would confine me to my room for a year!"

"But it's not a thing Love Ball Dotson's girl would do," Porter said. "Is it?"

That burned me up.

"I can do things, too!" I cried. "Why, I can be just as naughty as a boy when I want to!"

"Would you like to do naughty things sometimes?" Porter asked.

"Yes!"

"Why?"

"Because . . . because . . . I don't want to be Love Ball Dotson's good little girl all the time!"

"Who do you want to be? Woodrow maybe?"

"No! Me! Just me! And nobody sees me!"

"Why do you think they don't see you?" he said, leaning forward into the dim light.

We were eyeball-to-eyeball.

I couldn't find the right words.

"I see you," Porter said. "I can see you even under all that hair."

"What . . . what do you see?"

"Well, let's see. You remind me a whole lot of your Aunt Belle, the way you're so talented with music."

It was the second time that summer I had heard that, and it tickled me.

"And you're wonderfully imaginative and creative like her. But she was mad at the world because she wasn't Love. You're also a fine person in your own right. Nobody can outshine you if you can just be yourself. Belle never learned that, and it caused her a lot of grief."

"What do you think happened to her?" I said.

"Belle? Oh, that's easy. She actually vanished, you see, many years ago, when she was about your age. Now she is out there trying to find herself again."

Seventeen

For the rest of summer vacation things were not quite the same between me and Woodrow, but we were polite to each other. We didn't mention the change.

The last Saturday in August Mama took me to Bristol to shop for new clothes, like she did every year. I didn't ask Woodrow to go along, even though I knew he had never been there and he really wanted to go. I got dresses, skirts and sweaters, shoes, and a topper for cool fall mornings. We had lunch at an S&W cafeteria, and drove home late through the rolling hills of Abingdon and Lebanon. It was a beautiful drive. Just me and Mama. We had a good time.

Coal Station got its first stoplight, at the intersec-
tion of Residence and Main, and we all trekked down
there to see it—even Dawg.

Grandpa was in the market for a new car, so Woodrow went around singing car-commercial ditties.

> *What a joy to take the wheel*
> *In your brand-new Oldsmobile!*

And: *You gotta drive it to believe it*
          The Dodge for '55!

Also: *Ford! Ford! New kind of Ford!*
          Car of tomorrow by Ford!

Woodrow also had a new joke: "Name me two cars
that start with P."

Of course everybody said, "Plymouth and Pontiac."

And Woodrow would come back with "No, they
start with gas!"

The apples started falling. Summer was dying.

It looked like Cleveland was going to the World
Series.

And there were no new developments in the Belle
Prater case.

My old familiar nightmare came more often, but
with less horror. It didn't send me into hysterics any-

more. Sometimes I would wake up with a tear on my cheek, haunted by the memory of blood on the face of a dead animal. I would look out my open window at the stars at such times, and I could almost recall what it was the nightmare was trying to tell me— almost. The ugly thing seemed ready to come out and show itself to me.

School started back the day after Labor Day, and Woodrow and I advanced to the seventh grade. You couldn't call it high school yet, but it was in the same building as the high school, and we would be changing classes. On the first day Woodrow and I found out we were assigned to the same homeroom. Our teacher was new, a man from eastern Virginia. Neither of us had ever had a man teacher before.

Several of our classmates, including Buzz, Mary Lee, Franklin Delano, Flo, and Willy, were in our room again. We all sat there in new clothes before the bell rang, talking in hushed voices and sizing the teacher up. He was a middle-aged man with tiny blue eyes and a big red nose. He was wearing a long-sleeved shirt and a tie, which I thought was uncalled for in this heat. Already beads of sweat were popping out on his forehead.

I reckon each one of us was wondering what the school year would bring. I was secretly promising myself to make the honor roll every six weeks, which was nothing new for me. I always made the honor roll, and Mama always said, "That's my good girl." I wondered what she would say if I made straight C's? The bell interrupted my thoughts.

"Good morning, young men and women," the teacher said.

We pulled ourselves up to attention and tried to look the part.

"I am Mr. Collins, your homeroom and first-period English teacher."

Straightaway Woodrow wanted to know what was his relation to Floyd Collins, the poor man who got himself trapped in the Kentucky cave.

"None whatsoever," Mr. Collins replied. "Though I have read of that unfortunate man."

That was a new one on Woodrow. He never had heard tell of two people a-bearin' the same last name and being no kin a'tall. And he told Mr. Collins as much. Why, everybody knew a Prater was a Prater, a Honaker was a Honaker, and a Coleman was a Coleman, no matter where they lived. Same as a dog was a dog and a cat was a cat. You couldn't get away from it.

Sometimes it was hard to tell if Woodrow was putting you on or not.

"Well, perhaps somewhere in the far past," Mr. Collins conceded, "all Collinses did come from the same hoose."

"What's a 'hoose'?" Woodrow wanted to know.

"That's how they say 'house' in eastern Virginia," Franklin Delano said, giving us a short lesson in dialect. "My uncle lives in Fincastle, and out there they say 'aboot the hoose' instead of 'about the house.' "

That didn't bother Mr. Collins one bit. In fact, he said it was an amusing observation. I decided I was going to like him.

"I am new here," Mr. Collins went on. "Not only in your school, but in your town. I arrived in Coal Station only last week, and I'm staying at the Presbyterian Manse with the minister and his good wife.

"So I would like to start by learning some things about you and your families. Could we have some volunteers first?"

Of course Woodrow volunteered.

"My name is Woodrow Prater. I live with my granny and Grandpa Ball in a great big old two-story hoose . . ."

Woodrow paused and grinned at Mr. Collins, who grinned back at him.

". . . on Residence Street. We have . . ."

"He's Belle Prater's boy," Buzz interrupted. "Do you know about her, Mr. Collins?"

"No," Mr. Collins said. "I am not familiar with that name."

"Tell Mr. Collins, Woodrow," Buzz went on, with a devilish grin. "Tell about your mama disappearing into thin air and all."

Everybody looked at Woodrow. I saw a shadow of pain flit across his face. But he collected himself just like that.

"Good idea!" he said cheerfully. "It was like this, Mr. Collins. My mama, Belle Prater, learned the secrets of invisibility."

"I see," Mr. Collins said politely. "Go on."

"She wasn't like most grown folks. She was still a child in some ways. She wished on a star and played she had a fairy godmother—stuff like that. She made up swell stories for me about the little people. And she believed in magic. You have to believe, you know, to make the magic work for you."

Mr. Collins nodded.

"We saw this ad in the back of a *Red Ryder* comic book," Woodrow went on. "I remember there was a picture of Little Beaver on the front cover.

"And the ad said, 'Want to become invisible? Learn the formula of the gods. Order your invisible recipe today!' And it gave an address to order. I wanted it more'n Mama did.

" 'Order it, Mama,' I begged her. 'I want to learn how to be invisible.' 'Cause I thought it would be fun to go around the other kids at school and hear what they said, and go to them later and repeat it to them.

"So just for fun we ordered the recipe. It was only seventy-five cents, and we took it out of our carnival fund. That's another thing Mama liked—the carnival. We always went over to Grassy Lick when the carnival was there.

"Then our recipe came in the mail, and some of the things it called for were so outlandish—like a vulture's feather, a jack-in-the-pulpit petal, a squirrel's toenail, a quart of dew from a graveyard, a pint of mother's milk, a hair from the mustache of a man with a girl's name. She got that one, by the way, from old man Leslie Matney before he kicked the bucket. Spit from a baby no more'n two hours old, and I don't know what-all. I forget the rest.

"Anyhow, I lost interest because it was too complicated, but Mama was so curious her nose like to twitched out o' joint. She was determined to mix that brew. And she did.

"She plotted and planned and went skulking about the holler till she found all the ingredients she needed. And she stirred them up and let 'em steep for three days like it said.

"When Daddy complained about the smell, she told him she was making sauerkraut. If Daddy had been sober, he woulda knowed it wadn't the season for cabbage.

"Then, on the fourth day, I come home from school and Mama was nowhere . . . Well, she was somewhere, but nowhere that you could see. I searched the house and barn, and called and called her, but got no answer.

"So I went to the kitchen and sat down to a bowl of corn bread and milk, and I heard Mama say, 'I'm here, Woodrow. Right beside you.'

"I about swallowed my spoon.

" 'It's okay, Woodrow,' she said. 'I drunk only a little, so I'll be reappearing soon.'

"And I felt a rush of air on my arm like she was touching me.

" 'The more you drink, the longer you stay invisible,' she said. 'Maybe we'll drink some together and go visiting next Sunday. Won't that be fun?'

"And I said, 'Joe Palooka!'

"It was about all I could think of to say.

"Then she reappeared maybe an hour later, and she was so excited.

" 'Next time I'll drink more,' she said to me. 'Lots more. Just think, Woodrow, you can go to the show and to the carnival and not have to pay. And you can go on buses and trains, or ships, planes even! Why, you can go anywhere!'

"It was the next Sunday morning she disappeared, and we haven't seen or heard from her since."

Woodrow sat down abruptly.

Mr. Collins grinned. You could tell he didn't believe one word Woodrow had said, but he was going along with the story.

"And where, pray tell, do you think she went?" he said.

"New York City, probably," Woodrow said nonchalantly. "There's a doctor there who operates on crossed eyes and makes them straight. I know she'll send for me soon."

"What a lie!" Buzz hissed under his breath.

"You have quite an imagination, Woodrow," Mr. Collins said. "But let's remember the difference between fact and fantasy. Who's next?"

About three people volunteered and told their things before I raised my hand.

"I am Gypsy Arbutus Leemaster," I said, ". . . and I . . ."

"Beauty is a short name for Arbutus," Flo interrupted. "Don't you think it suits her, Mr. Collins?"

"Very much so," Mr. Collins agreed.

"Don't you think we should call her Beauty?" Flo went on sweetly.

I felt an angry flush creeping up my cheeks.

"I can play the piano!" I blurted out.

The class fell silent in surprise. I was agitated under their watchful gaze, but I felt like I had to say something about me—the me that was hidden under the golden hair.

"Woodrow can tell g-good st-stories," I stammered. "B-but I can tell good jokes. And I make good grades. And animals like me, and . . ."

My classmates seemed puzzled. I took several deep breaths and tried to calm down.

"So?" Buzz interjected rudely.

I saw Woodrow bristle.

"I live on Residence Street with my mother and stepfather, Porter Dotson," I concluded quickly and sat down.

"Porter Dotson?" Mr. Collins said. "Yes, he is one person I have met since I've been here. A very fine man."

"Not as fine as my real daddy!"

The words came out of nowhere.

"His name was Amos Leemaster. He died when I was five."

"Oh, I'm sorry, dear. Was it an accident?"

Suddenly my heart was pounding so hard I could feel it in my ears, and my mouth was so dry my lips stuck together. I pushed back my hair with shaking fingers and felt sweat trickling down the back of my neck.

"Yes, it was an accident," I said.

I glanced at Woodrow, and he gave me an encouraging smile.

"He was a volunteer fireman," I went on, and I could hear my voice trembling. "And . . . and he went into a burning house to save a baby, and . . . and he did save the baby, but he . . . he died."

"That's a lie!" Buzz Osborne said out loud.

"That's a very rude thing to say!" Mr. Collins scolded Buzz.

"Well, it *is* a lie. Let me tell you . . ."

"Shut up, Buzz!" Woodrow shouted.

I was gripped with terror. Buzz was going to say it. He was going to make me hear it.

"My mother said that Amos Leemaster got his face so scarred up in that fire you couldn't recognize him, and . . ."

"I said *shut up!*" Woodrow hollered, as he stood up and moved toward Buzz.

"Boys! Boys!" Mr. Collins tried to intervene, but his voice was drowned out by Buzz's next words.

". . . and he was married to the prettiest woman in the hills . . ."

"We do not talk about this in front of Gypsy!" Woodrow screamed, and raised his fist to Buzz.

"So he took a gun and shot his own self in the face!" Buzz continued. "Amos Leemaster killed himself!"

So there it was. The ugly thing was out.

Eighteen

There was talk for months about how Woodrow Prater beat the tar out of Buzz Osborne on the first day of school. But I was not there to see the fight. During all the commotion I left the classroom on wobbly legs.

I don't remember walking home.

Buzz's words had stunned me so that my mind was like a record with the needle stuck in a crack.

Shot in the face. Killed himself.

Shot in the face. Killed himself.

Of course I knew it all the time. I was there. I saw what happened. But how can you keep a thing like that in your head and go on talking and playing and eating and sleeping? It's a thing you can't look at every day, so you hide it away and pretend it never happened. You have to.

People were good enough not to keep reminding me. It was like a black hole we tiptoed around, being careful not to go too close to the edge, or to peep into it. Sometimes folks almost let it slip, and sometimes they said it in whispers behind my back. But as long as I didn't have to hear the hard, cruel words, I could go on tiptoeing around the edge of the black hole. Only, in my dreams the truth looked out at me through the lifeless eyes of the animal.

Oh, Daddy! Daddy! Why did you do it?

I was five years old, playing on Granny's porch after church while Mama and Granny fixed dinner. It was a beautiful Sunday in autumn. The hills were golden. The apples were almost gone, but their sweet aroma lingered in the air.

"Go fetch Daddy, Gypsy. Tell him dinner is ready," Mama called to me.

I skipped down the steps in my black patent-leather slippers and crossed the lawn to our house.

Daddy's car was there in the driveway. He had stayed home from church ever since the fire. He hardly went anywhere.

"Daddy . . . Daddy," I called to him in my baby singsong voice as I went through the house.

He was not in the living room or in the kitchen.

"*Come out, come out, wherever you are,*" *I called.*

I tried to open his and Mama's bedroom door, but it was locked.

"*Daddy?*"

I knocked.

There was no answer.

The house suddenly seemed so quiet I was afraid, so I ran back out on the front porch.

"*Daddy!*"

There was an eerie silence.

It seemed like a voice told me then to look into the bedroom window, which was there at the end of the porch. It was low and open, and a white curtain was blowing gently in the breeze.

Maybe Daddy was taking a nap.

So I looked in.

I could see only his head, face up there where he had fallen on the floor by the bed. It was in a puddle of blood.

Now seven years had passed. I entered my empty house again. Porter and Mama were both at work. I knew Granny and Grandpa next door were gone to Wytheville to see Granny's sister.

I went straight to my room and sat down on my vanity stool.

Oh, Daddy, why, why, why?

I looked at myself in the mirror.

"*Promise me you'll never cut my Beauty's hair.*"

"But look what *you* did!" I cried out at him.

An unspeakable rage began to rise in me.

"WHY DID YOU DO IT? I HATE YOU! I HATE YOU! YOU HAD NO RIGHT! I WISH I COULD HURT YOU THE WAY YOU HURT ME AND MAMA! I WISH I COULD KILL YOU! I WISH . . ."

The scissors were lying there on the dresser just like they were waiting for me. And with all my rage rushing into my hands I began to whack away at the golden hair.

Whack! Whack!

I gathered up long strands and cut it close to my head.

"WHY DID YOU DO IT!"

Whack! Whack!

Until it was all gone. Locks of hair lying in heaps on the hardwood floor. Nothing left on my head but ugly gaps and gashes and deep angry ridges. My scars were now visible.

I was gasping with exertion, but my anger was not spent.

"I HATE YOU, AMOS LEEMASTER! I HATE YOU!"

I rushed blindly out to the linen closet, fetched a sheet, and covered my mirror with it. I never wanted to see myself again. Beauty was no longer there. She had gone away.

"I am not your Beauty now!" I sneered at him.

Then I flopped down on my bed and stared at the

ceiling. My heart was hard and cold and miserable, but I had no remorse.

The telephone began to ring. I could hear it echoing through the empty house, but I would not answer it. I knew it was Mama calling from school. No doubt she had heard everything by now.

After a while I heard the front door open and close, and footsteps came down the hall. Somebody knocked on my door, but I didn't answer. My door opened and there stood Porter.

"Your mother asked me to find you," he said.

Then his eyes swept the scene—my head, the mess of hair on the floor, the sheet over the mirror.

"Go away," I said, and continued to look at the ceiling.

He didn't go.

"So you cut it all off?" he said calmly.

I didn't answer.

"Do you feel better?"

"No."

He sat down on my vanity stool and surveyed the damage.

"How *do* you feel?" he asked.

"Mean."

"Why? Because you did a naughty thing?"

"No, because my heart is so hard and cold. I don't care at all."

"About what?"

"About him! About anything!"

"Him? Who are you talking about?"

"You know! Amos Leemaster!"

"Oh, is that what this is all about?" Porter said.

I didn't answer, because I wasn't sure. Everything was mixed up.

"I don't want to be Mama's good little girl anymore, or Daddy's Beauty. I want to be ugly and evil!"

"But you are not ugly and evil," he said gently. "You never will be. You're wounded, that's all."

Wounded?

It was a word that touched a chord. I felt something give in my throat. A great choking sound came up from my chest. Porter moved toward me.

"Go away!" I screamed at him.

He halted.

"Okay," he said. "I'll go away. But you need to cry it out, Gypsy. It wants to come out."

He paused at the door. "I'll talk to your mother before she sees you."

Then he went out and closed the door behind him, but he didn't leave the house. He stayed somewhere near while I cried.

At first I cried only for me and all my years of pain and anger and grief. But then I cried for Mama and Aunt Belle, who loved him, too. Still, I couldn't bring myself to cry for Daddy, whose wonderful face had been scarred beyond repair. I couldn't forgive him for leaving us in the way he did.

Then a great weariness and a deep sadness settled over me, and I slept.

Nineteen

Mama took it fairly well, considering. Of course, Porter talked to her for a long time before he let her see me. I had the feeling he put his foot down. At one point I heard him raise his voice, "You'll do no such thing!"

And whatever it was, she didn't talk back. I had to admit things might have been lots worse without Porter on my side. When Mama finally did come to my room, she couldn't hide her disappointment, but she didn't fuss. She let out a pitiful whimper, then hugged me.

"We'll get it trimmed up evenly before you go back

to school," she said, as if my hair were the issue. "I'll not have the kids laughing at you."

"Mama, I want to talk about Daddy," I said quickly, before I lost my nerve. "We never have talked about . . . the way he died. I mean you and me . . . we haven't."

Such pain crossed her face I nearly took it back. But she spoke.

"He committed suicide, Gypsy."

It was almost a whisper.

"He shot himself in the face. What more is there to say? We didn't talk about it because we couldn't bear to. Take those nightmares of yours . . . remember how you would say, 'Why can't I see its face?'

"You just couldn't stand to look truth in the face, that's why. It was a tragic, tragic thing you had to see through the window that day. None of us will ever be quite the same again."

"Why did he do it?" I cried out. "Why?"

Mama paused, breathed deeply, and searched for the right words.

"He was in a deep depression. He couldn't accept his disfigurement. Do you remember that?"

"I remember he had scars after the fire, but he was my daddy. I loved him and I always saw him as handsome and wonderful."

"But that hasn't stopped you from being angry with him, has it, Gypsy?"

"Yeah, I've been real mad at him."

"Is that why you cut your hair?"

"I think so. I think I was trying to get back at him for what he did to us. But it was more than that, Mama. I don't know if I can explain it, but I felt invisible. The hair was like a veil or something that hid the real me."

I searched Mama's face for a hint of understanding. Suddenly she took on that long-ago look, exactly like Granny's.

"Belle used to say that same thing," she said softly. " 'Sometimes I feel invisible,' she would say. 'Nobody can see the real me.' "

"Are you disappointed in me, Mama?"

"Not much. Trying to keep that promise to your daddy was getting to be a real burden to both of us."

"How come it mattered so much to him how we looked?" I said.

"I'm afraid appearances were too important to your father," Mama said, sighing. "That's why the scars were such a crushing blow to him."

"Do you think I'll ever get over being mad at him?"

"Yes, you'll forgive him in time, just as I did."

Later Grandpa came over to see me in my room and brought me a big piece of chocolate cake and a glass of milk. He didn't even mention my hair, but he confided in me that Woodrow had thrashed Buzz soundly, and it was about time somebody did. We were proud of Woodrow, but we decided to keep it a secret, because you couldn't let a thing like that leak out.

Beginning that day Woodrow was confined to his room for two weeks for fighting at school. He could go out only to the john, to eat his meals, and to church and school. No phone calls or visitors. That was the hardest part for Woodrow.

For cutting my hair I voluntarily took on the same punishment for myself, partly because I wanted to hide anyway, and partly to show my support for Woodrow, who had tried to shield me from hurt.

That first night the sadness stayed with me. It sat on my chest like some dark parasite, feeding on my grief. I felt old. Tears would come suddenly and without warning. I tossed and turned all night long, then slept far into the morning the next day, which was Wednesday. Nobody disturbed me.

That evening Porter made arrangements to take me to Akers's Barbershop after hours when nobody else was around to see me.

"Don't worry none, Gypsy," Clint said, patting me on the shoulder as I slid into the barber chair. "I think I can fix it so it won't be so jagged. It's gonna be real short, though."

I shrugged, wondering what Porter had told him.

"You shore done a job on yourself, didn't you?" Clint went on. "I hope you don't ever get mad at me!"

Clint winked at Porter, then started in with his clippers. When he was finished, he turned my chair back to the mirror. I was startled. Somebody else was looking back at me. It was short, all right, but not that bad, just different.

"You might not believe this," Clint said kindly, interrupting my thoughts, "but in them fancy New York magazines, you see the models with this same cut. They call it the Pixie."

"Maybe we'll start a trend, Clint," I said, feeling slightly light-headed in more ways than one. "Everybody'll want a Gypsy Leemaster cut."

"Yeah, the Gypsy Pixie!" Clint said.

"Or maybe the Clint Cut!" Porter spoke up. "We'll run an ad for you in the *Echo*."

"In the Hick-o *Echo*?" I joined in. "Are you loco? We'll put it in the *Bristol Herald*!"

"Why stop there? Let's do *The New York Times*!" Porter said.

"The Dixie Pixie! That's it!" Clint said.

Porter and I laughed together. Fancy that—me and Porter.

"I'm serious, y'all," Clint said. "See, in New York it's called the Pixie, but in Coal Station, Virginia, it's the Dixie Pixie!"

We were joking around, of course, but when I went back to my solitary confinement, I started imagining myself at school tomorrow with all the stares and questions, and kids pointing at me and snickering be-hind my back. How could I explain? What could I say?

I dreaded the whole ordeal, and for the first time I regretted having cut my hair. Just like Aunt Belle, I had painted myself into a corner. Funny how people had been comparing me to her, and now I was doing it myself.

Impulsive—that was the word Mrs. Cooper had used for Aunt Belle. Yeah, you could say I had done an impulsive thing.

Then gradually a plan began to take shape up there under my new do. I got myself into this, now I would get myself out.

Twenty

"It's not all that bad," Woodrow said kindly—talking about my hair.

We were beginning the walk to school the next morning. I couldn't tell if he meant it or not. I glanced around nervously for other kids.

"I'm sorry you had to hear . . . those words from Buzz," Woodrow said.

"It's okay, Woodrow. I guess I needed to hear them. I can talk about it now."

"I didn't know all the details about your daddy, Gypsy," he said softly. "Granny told me last night. I'm sorry."

"What details? You knew he . . . how he died, didn't you?"

"Yeah, I knew that. But I didn't know you were the one who found him . . . like that. We were still so little then, both of us. Maybe that's why nobody ever told me anything. Mama never did want to talk about it."

I didn't answer.

"That day you got delirious at the movies, you kept hollering, 'Don't look in the window!' That's what you were remembering, I reckon?"

"I reckon. My mind was all muddled," I said.

"I used to think . . ." Woodrow went on. "Well, I was jealous of you because I thought you had it so easy. I thought . . . but I just didn't know how much you had been through . . . how you were hurt in-side . . ."

"From what I hear, cousin," I said, in an effort to change the subject, "between you and the chiggers, Buzz Osborne has not had a great summer."

Woodrow grinned sheepishly.

"That's right. You shoulda seen him blubbering and whimpering like a little puppy," he said.

"What did Mr. Collins do?"

"He wormed his way between us, but he was kinda slow in doing it, you know? I think he liked the way the fight was going. And he said . . ."

Here Woodrow stood still and took on a prim expression to do Mr. Collins.

" 'I am seriously disappointed in you. I was under the assumption that you were gentlemen!'

"By that time my fists were raw and Buzz was pretty well licked. So I said, 'Beggin' your pardon, Mr. Collins. I wouldn't spoil your first day on the job for nothing in the world, but this feller has been asking for it, so I finally give it to him.'

"Then he took us both to Mr. Cooper."

"Did . . . did any of the kids talk about me?" I asked hesitantly.

"Yeah. They all said it was real mean of Buzz to hurt your feelings like that, and they were glad I beat him up."

"Does anybody know about me . . . you know, whacking my hair off?"

"I don't think so. Nobody mentioned it at school yesterday, and I sure didn't tell anybody. They just wondered why you weren't there. But they'll know about your hair soon enough. Here comes Mary Lee."

She was coming out of her house as we approached.

"Hey, Woodrow! Hey—Gypsy! Is that you?"

She stopped in her tracks.

"Your hair . . . ?"

I took a deep breath and plunged right in. "I am just tickled to death with it!" I gushed.

Then I sashayed around so she could see it from all angles.

"It's called a Dixie Pixie!" I went on breathlessly. "The latest thing out of New York City!"

There was dead quiet except for the morning birds singing, as Mary Lee—and Woodrow, too—studied me with puzzlement on their faces.

Was this going to work?

"Why . . . it's really something," Mary Lee said at last. "A Dixie . . . ?"

"A Dixie Pixie! I just love it!" I said with all the enthusiasm I could muster.

"But all your pretty curls . . . ?" Mary Lee began.

"They were just too much of a burden!" I interrupted, using Mama's words. "I should have done this years ago."

Woodrow was still eyeing me.

Then here came Garnet and Willy. Practically the same exchange took place.

"I declare! I think I like it!" Garnet said. "I do! Who did it, Stella Smith at the Cut 'n' Curl?"

"Oh no. It has to be done by a real barber," I said nonchalantly.

"A barber? A man?"

"Yeah, sure. Clint Akers is the only one in this area qualified to do it. He's up on it. He reads the styling magazines, you know."

"Clint Akers?"

"Oh, yeah. He's the best."

"Clint? No foolin'?"

Then Peggy Sue fell in with us.

"For two cents I'd do mine like that," she said. "What's it called again?"

"The Dixie Pixie!" Mary Lee piped up. She knew all about it. "Just go in and tell Clint Akers you want a Dixie Pixie. He's up on it."

Yes! It was working!

I caught Woodrow's eye and gave him a quick wink. A funny smile was playing around the corners of his mouth, and I could almost hear him saying, "Nice goin', Gypsy."

I think in that moment I knew me and Woodrow would be friends for life. We had something. We understood each other.

I was bombarded as soon as I stepped foot on the school grounds. The word spread even faster than I thought it would. "Gypsy's hair" was the topic of the day. I managed to keep a level of excitement in my voice until I really was as tickled as I pretended to be.

"I was the first one she told," I heard Mary Lee say.

Occasionally Woodrow would drop a "Yeah" or "Ain't it the truth?" or something like that to back me up.

Then Patty Jo Blankenship, a popular tenth-grader, announced that she was going to the barbershop that very evening for a Dixie Pixie.

"It seems like such a modern thing to do!" she said.

"Me too!" June Lester agreed. "It's just the look I want."

Then Jewell Smith, whose mother was the afore-mentioned Stella Smith, beautician at the Cut 'n' Curl on Main Street, made me nervous for a second when she said, "What the heck is a Dixie . . . a what?"

Patty Jo explained, and Jewell said quickly, "Oh yeah. Sure. *That* Dixie Pixie. I know all about it. I thought you said something else."

The next day, Friday, six or seven girls, including Patty Jo and June, were sporting the new look, and about thirty others had plans to take the plunge over the weekend. It wasn't hard to figure out Clint's busi-ness was fixing to pick up.

I was elated.

I reckoned I was a different person in more ways than just my appearance, and a person who was any-thing but invisible.

Twenty-one

That night, as I lay reading a Nancy Drew in my room, Woodrow came whispering at my window.

"Gypsy!"

I looked out.

"The moon is full," he said. "Let's go on an adventure."

"An adventure? Woodrow, we're confined, remember?"

"So what? Turn out your light, and they'll think you're in bed asleep. Come on!"

"Where to?" I said.

"Everywhere. We're going with Blind Benny on his rounds."

In a second I was slipping jeans and a shirt over my shortie pajamas, and putting on socks and shoes.

Out by the street Blind Benny was waiting for us with Dawg.

"Hidy, Miz Beauty," he said to me as I came up beside him and spoke. "How is things with you?"

"I'm okay. Please call me Gypsy," I said.

"Why, shore, if it's what you want."

His face, even with its peculiar eyes, seemed happy and peaceful in the bright moonlight.

"Benny has new shoes," Woodrow said, and pointed to Benny's feet. "See?"

"Ain't they fine?" Benny said proudly.

He raised one foot, then the other, for my inspection.

"They are," I said. "They are wonderful shoes."

"Brand new. Boys down at the hardware bought 'em fer me," Blind Benny went on. "They seen I wuz pert near barefooted in my old ones with my toes a-sticking out. And they sez it's gonna be a cold winter. Woolly worms is wearing thick coats a'ready."

"Where we going to?" Woodrow asked, impatient to get started.

"Toward the station," said Benny. "We'll go down the tracks tonight."

Quietly but rapidly we set off down the street three abreast, with Benny holding on to Woodrow's arm.

"So's we can move faster," he explained. "When I

got nobody to hold on to, I hef to feel my way, and it slows me down considerable."

Hiccup, the Hickses' dog, and the Comptons' Sandy fell in step with Dawg behind us.

"Boys at the hardware is like family to me," Benny said. "I live in a room up over the store, y'know. I have your mama and pappy to thank for that, Gypsy."

"How's that?" I said, curious to know what business Mama would ever have with Blind Benny.

"Well, it beginned way back there in Cold Valley, Kentucky, a long time ago. I wuz borned like I am, don'tcha know, with hardly no eyes a'tall, and blind. My own mama and pappy, bless their hearts, died of the consumption when I wuz going on twelve. So I had nobody to keer fer me and give me food. That's how I got to be the sin eater."

"The what?" I said.

"Yeah. The sin eater. Don'tcha know about sin eatin', Gypsy?"

"No, what is it?"

"Well, it's this real old-timey backwoods tradition. And it goes like this: When a person dies, at the wake they take and spread out a banquet on his casket— all kinds of good eats. Then they call in the sin eater to eat the food.

"They say what happens is, all the dead person's sins goes into the food, and it's the sin eater's job to eat up the food and take the sins into his own sef, so the dead person can go to his glory clean and free."

"I never heard the beat!" I sputtered. "They made you do that?"

"They shore did. They always give the job of sin eatin' to somebody who's down on their luck and can't do no better. That were me in them hard days in Cold Valley. To look at how good I'm doing now, you'd never know I was a sin eater for nearabout fifteen years.

"The sin eater wuz always shunned and scorned by the town folks, 'cause I had all them sins inside me I had et, see? There weren't no more miserble person living than I wuz then. What got to bearing on my mind wuz who would eat poor old Blind Benny's sins when he passed on?

"Why nobody would, that's who! No matter how down and out a body might be, he wouldn't take the chance on eating the sin eater's sins. Which meant I would have to pass on when my time come with all them sins in me, and nobody to eat them for me.

"Then Amos Leemaster sez to me one day, 'Nonsense, Benny! That's what it is! A bunch of ignorant superstitious nonsense!'

"Them were his very words, and I shore was relieved to hear it from a man I respected and trusted. I believed him, and he took a load off'n my mind fer me.

"Then Amos sez I should go with him to Coal Station, Virginia, where nobody knew me, and start a brand-new life.

" 'I'm opening a hardware store there, Benny,' sez he. 'And you are welcome to come with me. I'll give you a room above the store and plenty to eat. You won't ever hef to eat sins again!'

"So that's how I come here fifteen years ago. I done all I could to hep out in the store, and in the volunteer fire department Amos started, too, but being blind and all, I weren't able to hep much.

"When Amos died, Love sold the store, but she put it in legal writin' that Blind Benny would always have a room at the hardware. 'Cause Amos promised. Nobody objected to that, and the new owners have been kind to me, too. I'm a lucky man."

How good it was of Mama and Daddy, I was thinking, to do what they did for Blind Benny and not brag about it one bit!

We reached the quiet coal yards, where the railroad cars were lined up neatly in the station, some full, some empty. You could smell the coal.

We headed down the railroad. You could see the steel tracks like deep blue ribbons stretching far and away through the valley in the moon's light, following Black River as it snaked between the hills. There was a cool breeze over this still, ghostly scene, and I knew all of it was carving an impression deep into my mind.

I would be able to call up this picture again and again whenever I wanted to see it. The memory is clever that way.

By the tracks there were houses anchored securely on the hillside. Here Benny moved in and out of the yards, feeling his way without a sound, to find his treasures. Woodrow and I watched curiously from the tracks while waiting for him.

Some people left things on their porches for Benny—worn-out clothing, coffee, potatoes, tobacco. These items he slipped into a pillowcase attached to his belt. Other useful things Benny found in the trash—an empty lard can, a newspaper, a piece of clothesline.

More dogs came up to us, nosing out me and Woodrow to see if we were acceptable. And finding us to be fairly decent critters, let us stay. They leapt about, greeting each other with endless sniffing and tail wagging and dog talk. You could tell they were old friends. I counted nine doggy heads.

Benny patted each one and called them by their names, though he couldn't tell you the names of their owners. I suspected he made up names as he went along.

We continued until we reached a long stretch where there were no houses at all.

"I smell a polecat," Benny said, as he stopped to sniff the air.

"Hope we don't run into him," Woodrow said. "Me and Gypsy might have a hard time explaining how we got sprayed by a polecat while we were supposed to be in bed asleep."

Benny chuckled. "We're safe," he said. "Even a panther wouldn't mess around with this pack o' dogs."

"Wanna hear a joke?" I said suddenly, as the railroad tracks reminded me of a good one.

Naturally they did.

"There were these two men, see, walking down the railroad tracks, when all of a sudden they came upon a human leg laying there on the tracks.

" 'O Lordy, Lordy,' said the first man. 'That looks like Joe's leg!'

" 'Yep!' said the second man. 'That *is* Joe's leg.'

"So they walked on and they came upon an arm.

" 'O Lordy, Lordy,' said the first man. 'That looks like Joe's arm!'

" 'Yep!' said the second man. 'That *is* Joe's arm.'

"So they walked on and they came upon a torso.

" 'O Lordy, Lordy,' said the first man. 'That looks like Joe's torso!'

" 'Yep!' said the second man. 'That *is* Joe's torso.'

"So they walked on and they came upon a head.

" 'O Lordy, Lordy,' said the first man. 'That looks like Joe's head.'

" 'Yep!' said the second man. 'That *is* Joe's head.'

"So the first man walked over and picked up the

head by its ears, see, looked it in the face, shook it, and hollered, 'Joe! Joe! Are you okay?' "

Well, that was a winner. We laughed till we couldn't laugh a bit more. It seemed like nothing ever had been so funny. And for years after, whenever me and Benny would chance to meet up again, he'd say to me, "Joe! Joe! Are you okay?"

The dogs trotted along happily at our heels like they were glad to be there with us even if we didn't have good sense.

My spirits soared. I felt like skipping except you can't skip on a railroad track. I wanted to sing, but Benny did it for me. He broke into song so smoothly it was like part of the natural night.

> *He was some mother's darling*
> *Some mother's son*
> *Once he was fair*
> *And once he was young*
>
> *Mary, she rocked him*
> *Her baby to sleep.*
> *Then they left him to die*
> *Like a tramp on the street.*

And I remembered something Mrs. Compton said to us in Sunday school one time. She said Jesus might come to us in disguise.

"He may be dressed in rags," she said. "He may be old and ugly. He may be diseased or crippled. So be careful how you treat people."

On down the tracks there was a huge rock jutting out of the bank and way over the river. We climbed out on it, helping Blind Benny along so's he wouldn't fall. The dogs nosed around the water's edge while we sat on the rock looking at the moon reflected in the water. There were billions of stars dancing between the mountaintops, and we could hear the water lapping gently against the bank.

A light breeze played with what was left of my hair. I ran my hand through it and marveled at the sensation. It felt like somebody else's head.

We were quiet, each in our own thoughts. At one point Woodrow took off his glasses to clean them on his shirttail, and I saw his profile clearly against the night sky.

Why, he looks for all the world like Prince Valiant! I thought.

Then Benny sang again:

> From this valley they say you are going,
> I shall miss your bright eyes and sweet smile;
> For they say you are taking the sunshine
> That has brightened our pathway awhile.

Won't you think of this valley you're leaving,
O how lonely, how sad it will be,
Do you think of the sad heart you're breaking,
And the grief you are causing me.

Come and sit by my side if you love me,
Do not hasten to bid me adieu;
But remember the Red River Valley,
And the one who has loved you so true.

"It's so sad," Woodrow said. "It reminds me of Mama."

"And it reminds me of Amos," Benny whispered. "I miss him every day still yet after all this time. He was the best friend I ever had."

"Me and Gypsy will be your friends, Benny," Woodrow said sweetly. "You just call on us the same as you did Uncle Amos whenever you need anything."

I thought I heard Benny sniffling.

About 2:00 a.m. we were dragging up Residence Street toward home, me and Woodrow worn to a frazzle. We had dropped off dogs one by one along the way. So the only one left was our beloved Dawg.

Benny was "working" our street then and his pouch was nearly full.

"This has been the most fun I ever had," Woodrow said.

"How 'bout you, Miz Beauty?" said Benny. "You had fun?"

Impulsively I stood on tiptoe and kissed him on the cheek right beneath his eye. I reckon nobody was more surprised than me.

"When I'm allowed to come back and live one day over again exactly as it was," I said, "this day will be considered."

We left him standing there in the moonlight with Dawg still by his side, and with one hand Benny was touching the spot I had kissed.

Sometimes impulsive is okay.

Twenty-two

"Therefore," Woodrow concluded the reading of his English assignment, "it is my belief that Blind Benny, even with his poor sightless eyes, is the only person I know who can see with perfect clarity. Because Benny is able to see beyond appearances."

"Excellent! Excellent!" came from Porter and Doc Dot as everyone applauded.

"A very wise observation" came from Granny.

"Wonderful, wonderful!" came from Mama and Irene Dotson.

"I would give it an A," said Grandpa.

"Keen!" came from me.

The twins, Dottie and DeeDee, just grinned and clapped.

It was another birthday dinner at our house—this time for Granny, and a somewhat special occasion because Porter had promised a couple of surprise announcements.

It was a Saturday night, still in September, and mine and Woodrow's confinement would be ending next Tuesday. We were given a temporary reprieve for this dinner. I suspected none of the adults cared if we observed our confinement rules anyway.

In school Mr. Collins had given us the assignment of writing a paper about a person we admire and why. I still had not done mine. Grandpa, having proofread Woodrow's paper, was so impressed he had insisted Woodrow read it at the birthday dinner.

Then Porter stood up, holding a glass of blackberry wine.

"I want to propose a special toast to Mother Ball, my good mother-in-law and granny to these children. Then I have an announcement. The toast first: Here's to a fine woman, wife, mother, homemaker, and a talented music teacher! We salute you, Mother Ball," he said.

"Hear! Hear!" the adults said, and drank a toast to Granny.

The little girls and Woodrow and I had cherry pop.

Granny blushed and thanked everybody.

"And now for the announcement," Porter went on. "It concerns your finest piano student, Mother Ball."

"Oh, Gypsy, of course," Granny said, beaming at me.

My ears perked up. What was this all about?

"We think it's time for Gypsy to have a formal recital."

"A recital?" I screeched. "What for?"

"What for?" Porter said. "To show off for us and for Coal Station."

"Show off?" I repeated like a dummy.

"Yes. Show off not only how good you are but to honor your teacher as well."

A recital? I was speechless. That meant just me all by myself playing the piano for about thirty to forty-five minutes in front of a bunch of people.

"I think your thirteenth birthday would be a perfect time," Mama said, looking very pleased. "That'll give you about two months to prepare."

"Who will we invite?" I asked.

"Everybody!" came from everybody at the table.

"Yeah, the whole town," said Woodrow.

They were all waiting for me to react. And surprisingly, I felt a thrill of excitement beginning to grow. I could show off all those tricky finger things I had learned, and all those beautiful Mozart pieces, the popular stuff, too, and the folk songs, and of course the jazz! A program was taking shape in my head.

"Joe Palooka!" I said breathlessly, unable to hide the excitement.

Then everybody laughed and applauded.

"We'll lay our plans tomorrow," Mama said.

"And now for that other announcement," Doc Dot declared, and stood up. "Regarding Woodrow."

"Me!" Woodrow said, and his voice broke.

He looked startled, and the rest of us tried not to notice.

"Is it about my mama?" he said.

"Oh no, son, I wish it were. But it's still something good. Sometime back, friends, I examined Woodrow's eyes. Since that time I have been in correspondence with a doctor friend of mine who is an eye specialist in Baltimore. So after some long discussions with Porter and Mr. Ball here, we have decided to take Woodrow to my friend in Baltimore and see what can be done for him."

"You mean an operation?" I said.

"Probably. We can't give any guarantees," Doc went on. "But from what I understand, the chances for a successful operation look promising."

Woodrow was speechless.

"Cat got your tongue, cousin?" I said, poking him playfully.

"No," he said at last. "I was just waiting to hear Granny holler, It's time to wake up now and get ready for school. 'Cause I know I'm dreaming."

What a night! What a party! It was by far the best one we ever had.

Twenty-three

On October 11, the one-year anniversary of Aunt Belle's disappearance, Woodrow came scratching at my window at 4:45 a.m. We had planned it all out the night before, but when I opened my eyes, I couldn't remember what I was supposed to do.

"The breeze at dawn has secrets to tell you," Woodrow whispered through the screen.

I sat up. Oh yeah, we were going to the tree house to watch the dawn come.

"Don't go back to sleep," he went on.

"You must ask for what you really want," I said sleepily, and swung my feet to the floor, pulling a blanket after me.

"*People are going back and forth across the doorsill /
where the two worlds touch,*" he continued.

"*The door is round and open,*" I whispered as I eased
the screen to the floor.

He helped me out the window, and I pulled the
blanket after me. He had one of his own. We headed
for the tree house.

"Smell the apples?" Woodrow whispered.

We paused and breathed deeply. It was a wonderful
thing to feel the dew under our bare feet and the wet
leaves brushing our cheeks and to smell the sweet
aroma of apples at the peak of their ripeness.

Grandpa didn't even have to try to sell the apples.
They sold themselves. They were famous in our neck
of the woods, and folks would come by with their own
baskets and pokes to buy the best Golden Delicious
apples in Virginia.

"It's true what they say about appearances being
deceiving," Woodrow said as we continued through
the orchard.

"How's that?" I whispered.

"When I first came here, the trees were all in
bloom. I never had seen anything so pretty, and I
thought nothing could ever hurt people who lived in
such a beautiful place. Now the summer is gone. The
apples are ripe, and I have learned . . . well, I have
learned a beautiful place can't shelter you from hurt
any more than a shack can."

We climbed up onto the tree-house porch, wrapped up in our blankets, lay back on the raw lumber, and listened to the birds just beginning to come awake. There was a touch of pale lavender on the tops of the mountains.

"Think of all the millions of dawns this old world has seen," Woodrow said. "But it will never be this same one again . . . or that same one when she left."

We could hear Blind Benny somewhere down the street singing "When the Moon Comes over the Mountain."

"It was exactly one year ago today," Woodrow said, "and I still wake up every morning wondering where she is waking up, what she is seeing. What is she thinking about? What will she eat for breakfast? What is she planning to do today? I miss her so much."

"I wish I had known her better, Woodrow," I said.

"Yeah, you woulda liked her lots, Gypsy. We made up that place I told you about. That place in the air behind our house. Mama and me, we made up lots of places and things. We used to talk about where the two worlds touch, and we told stories to each other about it. One day it was a world of fairies and uni-corns, and the next day it was a place where giants and dinosaurs would eat you up. And sometimes it was a magical place where all you had to do was ask for what you really wanted. But I knew all the time it wadn't real.

"When the sheriff investigated, he asked if any of her clothes were missing, and they weren't, but some of mine were. I didn't tell him that. She took a pair of my pants and a shirt, and . . ."

"She couldn't wear your clothes!" I said.

"Yeah, she could. If you'll remember, for the last few years I wore some of my daddy's and Uncle Russell's hand-me-downs and they were always too big. She could've wore them easy. And some of my socks and shoes were gone, too. And a cap. She could have put her hair up under it. And the thirty dollars we had saved for my eye operation—it was gone, too.

"I believe she went over the mountain to Grassy Lick dressed as a boy. That's why nobody noticed her over there. She probably hitched a ride with the carnival, which I know was pulling up and leaving that day. Maybe she got a job with them as an errand boy or something. It was just the kind of thing that would appeal to her."

"Woodrow, don't you think you should tell Mama and Granny and Grandpa all this just to set their minds at ease that nothing awful happened to her?"

"Yeah, I reckon I'll do that today, Gypsy. I couldn't do it before."

"And Uncle Everett," I said. "He should know, too."

"Yeah, I'll tell Daddy, too. But I don't think he cared as much about her as he let on. He was like the

farmer in the golden-hair story. His conscience bothered him more than anything else 'cause he wasn't
always good to her.

"I kept thinking she'd send me a message through
the ads. Just to let me know she was okay. She
could've done that. She knew I'd be watching those
ads every week. We always said it would be fun to
send messages through the ads.

"But she didn't. I didn't miss a one. I read them
every Sunday, and there never was one that looked
like it might've come from her to me. Not one!"

"She still might do it, Woodrow."

"No, she won't. She's gone. She won't ever look
back now. I've known it for a long time, but it don't
hurt as much as it used to."

Woodrow fell silent.

It was a moment, I reckon, when we both faced the
truth. Aunt Belle had left Woodrow on purpose just
like my daddy left me. Not because they didn't love
us. They did. But their pain was bigger than their love.

You had to forgive them for that.

Far away we could hear a mourning dove. It was
crying for us.

There were streaks of gold on the horizon, throwing
an eerie glow into the orchard.

"We are in that in-between place," Woodrow said,
"that fascinated Mama so much."

"Between what?" I said.

"Well, first we're between being kids and grown-ups, you know? Then we're in that time between summer and winter. And we're also in that moment when a new day is just peeping over the horizon."

His voice was fading away from me. I was in an in-between place of my own—that lucid place between sleeping and waking.

And I was watching my daddy come riding over Cold Mountain on a black horse. Tall and straight in the saddle he was. Dark and rugged as the hills. Nobody in Coal Station had ever seen the likes of him.

A 1997 *Boston Globe–Horn Book* Honor Book

Lily's Crossing

BY PATRICIA REILLY GIFF

Turn the page for two sample chapters from this

heartwarming story about summer, friendship, and growing up

in America during World War II.

On sale now wherever books are sold.

DELACORTE PRESS

0-385-32142-2

Excerpt from *Lily's Crossing* by Patricia Reilly Giff

Copyright © 1997 by Patricia Reilly Giff

Published by Delacorte Press
Bantam Doubleday Dell Publishing Group, Inc.
1540 Broadway, New York, New York 10036.

Chapter 4

Gram's house was the last one on the canal. "Where the ocean swoops in to fight with the bay," she always said.

Up on stilts, the house hung over the water. In the living room was a deep, soft couch, a radio on legs, and, this year, the damn piano taking up the whole side wall. In back was a square little kitchen. It had so many pots and pans, and bowls, and dishes, and mixers, and mashers, that there wasn't an inch of room left on the yellow counters. Most of the stuff was dusty. Gram hated to cook.

The two bedrooms were separated from the kitchen by long flowered curtains. One was Gram's, the other was Poppy's.

Lily was glad there wasn't a third bedroom. All summer she slept on the porch that was tacked on the front. She was so close to the water beneath, she could lean over in her bed and watch the silver killies zigzagging along just under the dark surface.

Sometimes she looked up at the Big Dipper, but most of the time, like tonight, she watched the searchlights crisscrossing overhead. She knew the spotters were looking for enemy planes that might come all the way from Germany to bomb New York.

And suppose she was the one to spot a plane and bombs coming down? She thought about it, diving through bombs to rescue the neighbors. She closed her eyes. Germans parachuting into the canal. She'd have to row like crazy, zigzagging away from the bombs, away from the paratroopers. It made her dizzy to think about it.

She listened. Something was going on. Noise. Lights. At Mrs. Orban's, four houses down. Yes, lights. Mrs. Orban hadn't even bothered to pull the blackout curtains, and the Nazis could zero right in with Lily two seconds away.

And right now, a car was driving up on the road side of the Orbans' house. Lily knelt up in bed and leaned against the screen. Never mind that Gram had told her a hundred times she was going to knock the screen out and go headfirst into the water.

"Mr. Orban's Model A Ford," she said aloud. She knew that because she had helped him paint the top half of the headlights black so they couldn't be seen from the sky. The light Mr. Orban had painted had turned out much better than the one she had worked on.

Lily reached for her shorts and sneakers. She'd just get herself down there and find out what was going on. She wasn't one bit sleepy yet, anyway.

Strange that Mr. Orban was using the last drop of his gas. He had sworn he was going to hold on to it until the day when the war was over in Europe. "Then you and I, Lily my love, are going to drive up and down Cross Bay Boulevard," he had said. "We'll honk the horn every inch of the way."

She thought about sneaking out through the kitchen, but Gram would be awake in a flash. Instead she unhooked the screen and pushed it until it swung out.

Noisy, much too noisy. She counted to fifty, then wiggled through the opening and hung on to the window ledge until she felt the piling with her feet. The rowboat was directly underneath. She let go and landed on one of the oars.

For a minute she rocked back and forth holding her leg,

feeling the pain shooting down her shin. Tomorrow she'd have a black-and-blue mark the size of a potato.

The boat was rocking too, water sloshing in over the side. She could hear Mrs. Orban's back door opening, and the sound of voices, but they were too far away for her to know what they were saying.

Lily pulled the thick rope over the hook, setting the boat free. Then she pushed herself along under the porches, moving from piling to piling, not bothering with the oars.

She looked up as she passed slowly under the Colgans', the Graveses', the Temples'. Narrow slits of light from the sides of their blackout shades were reflected out onto the water, sliding up and down with the tiny waves.

Under the Orbans' porch, everything was still except for a gentle swish and the boat bumping against the pilings. The voices had stopped.

Lily sat there shivering, wishing she had brought her sweater. She wondered how long she should stay there. If she boosted herself up on the piling, quietly, carefully, she could grab on to the edge of the porch. The Orbans' porch was a plain open one, not like hers, which had been made into a bedroom. She could tiptoe across it and see into the kitchen window. She thought about it for a moment.

Gram said her whole trouble was she didn't think about things long enough. Of course she did. She thought all the time, about writing stories, and about the war, and about coming to Rockaway every summer. And she thought about her mother. Hadn't she brought a star every year to paste in back of her bed so her mother would be there in Rockaway too? Of course, Gram didn't know that. That was private stuff; no one knew, not even Poppy. Especially not Poppy. His face would get that soft look, that sad look.

Lily reached for the dripping rope and looped it over the Orbans' hook. All she needed was for the boat to float away without her. She slid the oars under the seats on one side. One almost broken shin was enough for tonight. Then she pulled herself up, hanging on to the rough floorboards of the porch.

She left a trail of wet sneaker prints going across, but they'd be dry before morning. And then she was under the window, and Mrs. Orban was talking again, talking a blue streak in her high voice, and Mr. Orban was talking too, a rumble of sound.

Lily crouched there, listening, catching bits and pieces. "Budapest . . . so far away," Mrs. Orban was saying, "but never mind . . . safe and sound . . . the beach . . . swimming . . ." Her voice trailed off.

"Maybe you'd like applesauce," Mr. Orban put in. "Or toast . . . margarine on it, though . . . butter's gone . . ."

"Andrassy Street," Mrs. Orban said. "I remember the cobblestones, and Kalocsa's Restaurant . . ."

5

"How about toast with applesauce on the side?" Mr. Orban asked. "What do you say, Albert?"

Albert? Who was that, now? Lily leaned back against the house to look at her leg. In the light from the window, she could see it was a mess.

Albert wasn't talking, not a word. Lily listened to Mr. Orban complaining that you had to be a genius to make the can opener work, while Mrs. Orban kept going on about the beach.

Then Lily heard her own name, clear as a bell. Lily Mollahan. Albert, whoever he was, was supposed to meet her, and they were going to be friends, Mrs. Orban was saying.

Lily knelt up slowly, so slowly it was as if she were swimming underwater. She gripped the edge of the windowsill with the tips of her fingers, then raised her head just high enough to see inside, and to hear clearly. And what she heard was Albert saying he didn't have time to be friends with any Lily Mollahan, saying her name in a strange, soft way, with an accent. "I have to find Ruth," he said.

What was he doing there, she wondered, sitting at the table directly across from her, a dish of applesauce in front of him, the skinniest kid she had ever seen in her life. His hair was curly and thick, but it looked as if he hadn't combed it in a hundred years. She stared at him, his face down in the shadows. A nice face, she thought, even though he didn't want to be friends. Too bad for him. She didn't want to be friends either.

He was wearing shorts, and his knees were big and knobby under the table, his legs like sticks. Then he looked up. His eyes were blue, the bluest she had ever seen, and he was looking straight into her eyes. He picked up his spoon, a little applesauce dripping off the edge, and, still staring, pointed it at her.

She could feel the heat in her face, and in her neck. Mr. and Mrs. Orban were turning toward the window, trying to see what he was looking at outside. Lily scrambled across the porch on her knees, and down over the edge, hanging on for a second, landing in the boat, grabbing the rope off the hook as fast as she could. She pushed herself back down under the porches so quickly she could hear the water churning up in back of her.

She didn't stop until she was in her bed with the red quilt pulled up to her chin. She lay there thinking about Albert—his blue eyes staring at her—and wondering who Ruth was. She couldn't believe she had been caught like that, sneaking around on the Orbans' porch in the middle of the night.

Chapter 5

Lily had been wandering around all of yesterday and today, trying to get another look at Albert. She wore the sailor hat Eddie Dillon had given her last summer, her sunglasses, and a thick layer of Victory Red lipstick from Gertz Department Store, FREE TAKE ONE. Albert wouldn't recognize her in a hundred years.

It didn't make any difference. Once she thought she saw him climbing around on the rock jetties at the beach, and once on Cross Bay Boulevard. But both times he was gone by the time she got close enough for a good look.

Right now it was Friday afternoon, late, and Poppy was finally coming for a weekend. In the rowboat, Lily dipped the oars into the water as quietly as she could. Any minute Gram would be after her to practice the piano, Etude in Something or Other, set the table for dinner, and who knew what else.

"Lil-y."

Too late.

Above her, the screen door opened.

Lily began to row, singing, " 'Mairzy doats . . . ,' " pretending she hadn't heard.

Gram wasn't fooled. "You could set the table, Lily," she called, "get everything ready before your father comes."

"Going to pick him up in the boat right now," Lily said over her shoulder. "Then he won't have to walk around the long way."

"And what about the piano?"

Gram was in love with that piano.

"Did you practice?" Gram began.

"This morning." She hadn't bothered much with the étude, she'd done the C scale twice, two minutes, and that was that. She began to sing again, " 'A kiddley divy too,' " listening for the sound of the door, but it didn't close. Gram was still standing there, waiting for her to turn around and come back.

Lily raised the oars, water plinking off the ends, but Gram didn't say anything.

"Going to get Poppy," she said again.

In back of her the screen door closed.

Lily dipped the oars into the water again, veering toward the railway station, hurrying now, anxious to see him.

The railroad trestle looped across the bay, flat against the water. Lily bent over the oars, wondering what Poppy would tell her about on the way back . . . probably how hot it was in St. Albans and how much he missed her. She smiled to herself, thinking about it.

She saw the smoke from the engine before she spotted the train. A moment later, it pulled into the station, and a knot of people piled out the doors. And there was her father, waving his newspaper at her. She waved back, rowing fast toward the dock, watching the distance narrow, angling around another boat that was coming in to meet the train. Then finally she rammed into the rough wood of the piling. She held the boat steady, stroking, until Poppy untied his shoes, pulled them off, and hopped in.

"Want to row?" she asked, leaning across for his kiss.

He shook his head, smiling, the lines around his eyes crinkling. She reached out to touch them with her fingers.

"Go the long way," he said, "around the trestle."

She knew Gram was waiting, broiling flounder, using the last dot of butter for little round potatoes, but she was so happy to be there with him, she didn't say anything.

She dipped the oars into the water, pulling slowly, evenly, watching him. He tipped his hat back and closed his eyes. "This is my favorite place," he said. "It's home, even though it's only for the summer."

Lily nodded. Tomorrow they'd line up at the deep-sea fishing dock, to climb aboard the *Mary L.* before the sun came up. They'd fish all day, the boat smelling of kerosene and heat.

Tomorrow night, she and Poppy would walk to the Cross Bay Theatre. He loved the movies too. It would be her fourth time for *Fair Stood the Wind for France*, first time paying. Then on Sunday, after Mass, they'd read, finish *Evangeline* or . . .

"I have to tell you . . ." Poppy's eyes were open now, blue with paler flecks of gray, his face suddenly serious.

"The Dillons left for Detroit," she said quickly. "Mr. Dillon's going to be a foreman in a factory in charge of making planes. Top secret, Margaret says."

Poppy grinned. "It won't be top secret for long, not if Margaret knows about it."

Lily swallowed, watching him smile.

He reached out, put his hand on the oars. "I have to go too. I came tonight to tell you."

She didn't look at him. "To a factory like the Dillons? When would we leave?"

She looked out across the water, seeing him shake his head from the corner of her eye.

"The army needs engineers," Poppy said.

For a moment she felt as if she couldn't breathe. "Who's going to take care of me?"

"Gram," he said. "Gram, of course."

Gram. She closed her mouth over the word, didn't want to hear it. She and Gram all alone in St. Albans this winter, the wind rattling around the house.

"Please," she said, but she didn't even know if she had said it aloud.

Poppy put his hand over hers. "Listen. People are being killed just for disagreeing with the Nazis, or being Jewish."

"I'm sick of the war," she said.

"It's going to be over someday," he said, "now that the Allies have landed in France."

She shook her head. "It'll take forever."

Poppy sighed. "There's been nothing but destruction in this war, families separated, villages ruined, cathedrals bombed . . ."

She opened her mouth, trying to think of something to say, something that would change his mind.

"But right behind the armies will be people like me," he said. "The engineers, the builders. We're the ones who'll help put Europe back together again."

"Where will you go? When . . ."

He shook his head. "It could be anywhere. England, maybe, or Germany."

"I won't even know where you are."

"Yes, you will," he said.

Lily shook her head. "Mrs. Colgan doesn't know where her brother is. She said the censors cross everything out in the letters. She can't even guess what country."

Poppy squeezed her hand. "That's true. But I promise, I'll find a way to let you know, somehow."

Gram was calling now. She could hear her voice across the water. "Jerry, Lily, hurry."

"I love you, Lily," Poppy said. "I love you more than Rockaway. More than anything."

Lily edged the boat toward the dock. Gram was outside, her hand cupped over her eyes, watching for them.

"What will Gram say?" Lily asked. "She won't like it. She'll hate it. I know she will."

Poppy moved his hand, held it over Lily's wrist on the oar. "Gram knows."

Lily stared at him. "You told Gram first. You knew about it. Both of you keeping a secret . . . not telling me . . ."

She shook his hand off her wrist, feeling tears hot in her eyes, a terrible burning in her throat, feeling angry enough to burst. She hated him, hated Gram.

She started to row.

"Lily," her father began, then stopped.

She nosed the boat in under the porch, banging hard into the piling. She must have chipped a piece of paint off the boat, a couple of pieces. She didn't care, didn't care about one thing.

Poppy reached out to help her up, but she pulled away from him.

Gram was standing at the edge of the ramp that led to the kitchen, smiling a little, looking anxious at the same time. "You told her? I thought you were going to wait until after—"

"Mind your business," Lily said, and said it again. The words came out of her mouth so fast, they ran together. Then she ran up the path, away from the house. She wanted to go back to the water, but she'd have to pass them. Instead she went along the road, running on the tar, which was gluey from today's sun. She saw Albert and veered away from him, but she knew he had seen her too. He was standing in front of the Orbans' house, watching her cry.